Covid Attack

Brad Bacom

TotalRecall Publications, Inc.
1103 Middlecreek
Friendswood, Texas 77546
281-992-3131 281-482-5390 Fax
www.mousegate.com

Cover design by:. Bruce Moran

ISBN: 978-1-64883-066-2
UPC: 6-43977-40662-0
Library of Congress Control Number:
Printed in the United States of America with simultaneous printings in Australia, Canada, and United Kingdom.

FIRST EDITION
1 2 3 4 5 6 7 8 9 10

To Melanie
Thank you for your dedication and faith in me, for putting up with me and encouraging me to keep writing. Thank you for ignoring me when it's three in the morning and the sounds of the keyboard float throughout the house.

To Sunshine
Thank you for your keen eye and your ability to easily see my mistakes and the ability to recommend changes as needed.

Authors Bio

Brad Bacom spent the first half of his adult life as a cop in southeast Texas. The second half he spent as a part time cop and a private investigator, active in professional associations and writing for law enforcement and private investigation trade journals. He was involved in writing two novels when the Covid 19 pandemic hit and noticed a barely mentioned fact that a Harvard professor was arrested for selling U. S. secrets to two Chinese spies, one of whom was a lieutenant in the People's Liberation Army assigned to a lab at the Wuhan University of Science and Technology, ground zero for the pandemic.

About the Book

Covid Attack tells the story of how an extremely dangerous virus escapes from a secret lab beneath the chemistry building at the Wuhan University of Science and Technology. The escape triggers the virus which immediately begins to infect people in and near Wuhan. Withing weeks the virus becomes a pandemic that is sweeping the whole world.

Assistant Special Agent in charge of the Chicago FBI office, Chris Weber, arrests a Chinese spy assigned to the operations of China's secret lab. His partner is also arrested. When the FBI agents discover a hidden room in his house, they enter the room, triggering a bomb which blows up the house, the houses on either side, and the rookie FBI Agent on guard outside

Chris Weber is drawn into a task force called "Mongoose" run by a shadowy figure called "The General", the leader of the task force which includes several CIA spies in China, several FBI agents in the U. S. and The General, whoever he really is.

CHAPTER 1

Wuhan, Hubei District, China
October 14, 2019
3:22 pm, China Standard Time

The young Chinese peasant stood beside Luoshi S Road looking across to the China Wuhan University of Science and Technology. In his hand he held a piece of paper bearing the name and address of a man at the university who might be able to help him get a job there. Zhuang Wei, holding the paper in his hand, crossed the street at the light and walked into the campus. Using a map he bought at a local pancake house, he found the science building. Once inside, he found the chemistry department where he asked the receptionist where he might find Mr. Wang Lei. The receptionist called to a young man sitting nearby. When the young man came to her desk, she told him, "Escort this gentleman through the building and out the back door to find Mr. Wang Lei. Do you know who he is?"

"I do", the young man said. "Is he not the janitor who sits behind the building sometimes?"

"That is correct," the young lady answered. The young man said to Zhuang, "Please follow me. I will escort you to Wang Lei." Without waiting for a reply, the young man turned and began walking through the main corridor of the building. In a matter of minutes, the two left the building by the back door. There the young man introduced Zhuang to Wang Lei, the janitor for the chemistry department.

Wang was a stout man of about sixty years sitting on an overturned waste basket behind the building. The young man told Zhuang that, because it was late in the day, Wang would soon start his workday. Zhuang introduced himself to Wang who stood to shake his hand. Zhuang said, "My grandfather was a friend of your late grandfather who told us you were a man of some importance here at the university. My family is poor, and I have had to leave our farm to come to the city in search of a job. Is it possible you are looking for an assistant in your duties here?"

Wang studied the stoop-shouldered young peasant before him. His clothes were worn and patched but ironed and exceptionally clean. He wore typical peasant sandals, covered with dust, and carried a torn backpack over one shoulder. His hair was a little long and had obviously been cut at home with a pair of dull scissors. Wang noticed the small scar above his left eye.

"What is it you are qualified to do, young man?"

"I am only qualified to do manual labor," Zhuang answered. "I was raised on our farm where there is always plenty of hard work to be done. Perhaps someday I will be as qualified as you are, to be the head janitor for the chemistry department, but for now, I am willing to work hard and follow instructions if you are prepared to teach me. I am not very smart, but I can learn."

Wang said, "How did your grandfather come to know mine?"

Zhuang answered, "The two of them served together in the Red Guard during our glorious revolution. Oh, the stories your grandfather and my grandfather told me of the wonderful things the soldiers did back then! There was one other grandfather in our village who served with them, but I cannot remember his name. He died when I was a child."

Wang asked, "Was it Zin Li?"

"Yes, that is it," Zhuang said excitedly. "The three of them were always willing to share their stories when we were children. I so wanted to be in the Red Guard when I grew to be a man, but, alas, things are so different now."

Wang sat on his waste basket again. "Oh, I know. So much is different. The economy is so different and there are so many opportunities to work and earn a living and be able to send money home to our families. He reached behind him and produced another waste basket. He turned it over and set it close to him. "Please. Sit."

The two men sat and discussed China in general and Wuhan in particular. Wang said, "If I hire you, where will you live?"

"I do not know yet. I have only arrived in the city today. I shall look for a place to stay tonight."

Wang said, "It would be rude of me to refuse to hire the grandson of my late grandfather's friend. Follow me." Wang led him to a small metal shack just around the corner from where they had been sitting. He showed Zhuang the inside of a small shop where there was a single metal bed, a sink, and a toilet. "You may sleep here until you have enough money from your paycheck to rent a place of your own. I go home every night to my wife and children, so no one is using this bed now."

Zhuang asked, "Does this mean I am hired to work for you?"

"It does," Wang said. "How can I not hire a man whose best reference is that he is the grandson of my grandfather's closest friend?" Wang explained the duties and the pay to Zhuang.

"When may I start work?"

"You may start today. In a few moments, a bell will ring, and the workers and the students will leave the building, and I shall escort you inside and show you where you will work."

While Wang was still talking, a bell sounded for five seconds. Immediately a flood of people began walking out of the building and in ten minutes the flood had slowed to a trickle. In another two, the trickle stopped.

"Follow me," Wang said. He walked through the classrooms, the chemistry labs, the offices, and the restrooms. They neared a door with a sign which said "Basement" and Zhuang tried to open it. Wang said, "One cannot open this door without an electronic door key. This is mine." Wang pulled his ID card from his pocket and swiped it through the card reader beside the door. There was a buzz and the door opened about an inch. Wang immediately grabbed the door and pushed it closed again. "However," he said, "you are not allowed in the basement. Perhaps later you will be. I am the only janitor allowed down there."

"What is down there?" Zhuang asked.

"There is a lab there where government scientists are doing research. I do not know what they are researching. Nor do I care," he laughed. "I just go down there to empty wastebaskets and clean up their messes."

"It must be wonderful to be so smart and to know so many things about this university. I do not think I will ever be smart enough to do what you do and to know what you know." The two men continued their walking tour of the chemistry department and Zhuang made mental notes of each part of the lab, especially the door to the lower levels which was his main target.

After Zhuang had worked there five days, Wang approached him while he was cleaning a restroom. "Tonight," Wang said, "we must dispose of some dead pigs. Every Friday, the scientists conduct tests on three pigs. Apparently, the tests kill all three and, late in the evening, it is my job to dispose of the three carcasses. I get the keys to a truck before everyone leaves and later, I back it up to the door, load the pigs using the winch and drive them away."

Wang looked around to make sure no one was near, then said quietly, "I am required to load them into the incinerator and stay there until they are completely burned. However, I take the pigs to the market center where my brother has a butcher shop. He pays me a little for the pigs. I shall share the money with you if you are willing to help me and stay silent about our little business venture."

"I am willing," Zhuang said. "And I can use the extra money."

An hour later, the two men were on their way to the central market area of Wuhan with three dead pigs in the back of the truck covered with a tarp. Zhuang asked, "Why are the pigs killed?"

"I have no idea. Sometimes on a Friday I hear three gunshots, then I know the pigs are ready to leave."

In five minutes, they were stopped in front of a meat market at the center of the market district. When Wang stopped the truck, two men came out and pulled the tarp from the pigs. The two men carried all three pigs inside. After the last pig was inside, another man came out and embraced Wang, then stood staring at Zhuang. Wang said, "This is my new assistant of whom I spoke. He will help me load and transport the pigs. Sometimes I may just send him alone to make the delivery."

The man counted out money to Wang and returned to the market without uttering a word. Wang counted the money and gave half to Zhuang. Zhuang counted his share and saw it was about half of his weekly pay. The two men returned to the university where they parked the truck and continued their regular duties.

The next day, Zhuang talked with Wang about the beautiful sights in the city of Wuhan. Zhuang asked him, "Are we allowed to take photographs of these sights?"

"Yes, surely," Wang said, "but first, look closely for any sign which forbids photographs. They will be prominently displayed, so you cannot miss them."

Zhuang spent his next day-off taking pictures in and near the campus. He learned the students called it "The University in the Trees" because most of the buildings were hidden from sight by the overhead canopy of trees. He suspected this was intentional to foil enemy satellites. He had seen the satellite photos of the campus, especially the building where the chemistry lab was located. The overhead canopy of trees was obscuring much of the campus.

When Zhuang returned from his day off, he found Wang sitting in his usual spot waiting for the population of the building to go home. While they waited, he told Wang, "I think I shall make some tea. Would you care for a cup?"

"I would," Wang said. "Thank you."

Zhuang walked to the little metal building and turned on his hot plate. When the tea had been brewed and steeped, he removed a small plastic vial from his pocket. He unscrewed the cap and emptied the contents into Wang's cup. He stirred it until he was sure there was no residue showing then carried both cups out to the sitting area. He gave Wang one cup and sat on his own wastebasket. In ten minutes, the bell rang, and Wang upended his tea and stood. "Would you like for me to return your cup to the shop?"

"I would," Zhuang said, "and thank you."

The next afternoon when Zhuang returned for work, Wang was not there. As he sat on his wastebasket waiting for Wang to appear, a tall man with close-cropped hair came out of the building and approached him. "Are you Zhuang?"

Zhuang stood and said, "I am, Sir. How may I help you?"

"Come with me," the man said and immediately turned and walked down the hall. When they arrived at the basement door, the man used his ID card to open it, and Zhuang followed him inside. They walked down two flights of metal stairs and into an office marked "Lieutenant Qui." The man went in and sat, motioning for Zhuang to do the same.

He said, "Mr. Wang is in hospital. His wife called about an hour ago and said he has food poisoning and will be in the hospital several days. Until he returns, you must do your work and his. There are few replacement janitors we can use. Have you been down here before?"

"No, Sir. Mr. Wang told me I was not allowed down here," Zhuang said, looking around the spacious office.

"He was right to tell you that." He handed Zhuang an electronic key. "Unfortunately, until he returns, we must allow you down here to clean the place. Do you know what to do here?"

"No, Sir."

The man stood and said, "Follow me." He led Zhuang down a long hallway to a narrow room which was cluttered with electronic equipment. "This part of the lab is still being constructed. The workmen are required to clean up every day before they leave. However, they sometimes 'forget' to do so.

Every day you must come in here and, if necessary, sweep and mop the floors and dust the desks.

"Other than that, you must empty the wastebaskets and put all the papers from the collection waste boxes into the shredder outside my office. Do you understand your instructions?"

Zhuang said, "I do, Sir."

"Good. And you may not discuss with anyone what you see or hear down here. Is that clear?"

"It is, Sir."

Qui barked, "Any questions?"

"Just one, Sir," Zhuang said. "What do the people do down here with all this equipment and am I supposed to clean the equipment?"

"No," he said, "you do not touch the equipment and what we do down here is certainly not any of your business. Why did you ask that question?"

Zhuang answered, "I am trying to learn so that someday I might become as smart as Mr. Wang and be better at my job."

Qui looked at him for a moment and then made a face like Zhuang was a simpleton. He said, "That is the first time anyone asked such a question." As he climbed the stairs, Zhuang thought to himself, "And I bet that is the first time you have invited a CIA spy into a secret lab and given him a key to the place." He smiled as he climbed.

CHAPTER 2

Wuhan, Hubei District, China
October 15, 2019
8:32 am, China Standard Time

The next day, Lt. Qui Din Wa of the Chinese Peoples' Army knocked on an unmarked door in the basement of the chemistry building. When Colonel Husan Ling said, "Enter", Qui came in and sat down. Colonel Husan said, "Did you talk to the janitor?"

"I did," Qui said.

"What do you think?"

Qui said, "I think we have finally found the one man in China who is more stupid than our regular janitor."

"Will he fit the job?" Husan asked.

"I am sure he will. He is interested in learning what he can from Mr. Wang so that he can be as smart as Wang," Qui said with a chuckle.

"As smart as Wang? Our janitor Wang?" Both men laughed. Husan asked, "Did you make contact with anyone back in his village, in Sho Ping?"

"No, Sir. I finally discovered the name is actually Zhaopan. It is an exceedingly small village about 100 kilometers northwest on the G 70. He didn't even know how to spell the name of his own village. There is a catfish farm there and the owner of the farm, Mr. Chung, is also the town magistrate. He said Zhuang sometimes works for him during his busy season, seasonal work. He described him as a good worker, but in his words, 'dumb as a brick'. He said the boy takes great pride in his work with his limited intelligence. He is basically a farmer on his parents' farm."

Husan asked, "Did you get a good description of him?"

"I did," Qui said. "Right down to the small scar above his left eye. I am satisfied."

"Good," Husan said. "What is the latest news on Mr. Wang's health?"

"I went to the hospital this morning on the guise of checking on him. He is very sick. He retched the entire time I was there. He is pale, has a mild fever and has begun to lose weight. It is my opinion he is legitimately ill. I do not think he could fake that," Qui said.

As Qui and Husan were talking, Zhuang, secluded in his little tin hut and out of ear shot of the Chinese Army investigators, lay on his bunk contemplating his deception. When his cell phone rang, he retrieved it from under his mattress and closed the door to his shed. "Zhuang here."

"It is Chung. You were correct. A lieutenant named Qui called me last evening. He said he is assigned to the university in Wuhan and was checking references on a man named Zhuang Wei. I told him what you instructed me to tell him, and we both had a laugh about how stupid you are." He laughed. "I described your looks to him, concentrating on the little scar above your left eye. He seemed to be satisfied."

"Thank you," Zhuang said. "Very soon someone will arrive with your…reward," and disconnected.

Two days later, when Zhuang arrived for work, he was summoned by a lab assistant to Lieutenant Qui's office. He knocked and waited for the lieutenant to say "Enter", then went inside. The lieutenant said, "Please sit down, Mr. Zhuang." When he sat, Qui said, "I fear I have some distressing news to share with you today, Mr. Zhuang. I received a telephone call this morning from Mr. Wang's wife. Mr. Wang died during the night."

Zhuang sat back in his chair with a worried look on his face. "I am so sorry to hear that, Lieutenant. I really liked Mr. Wang and he was teaching me so much."

Qui said, "I know this is shocking news for you Zhuang, but it seems what was first thought to be food poisoning was actually a peptic ulcer. In effect, Mr. Wang bled to death internally."

"Does this mean, Sir, I will lose my job here since he will not be able to teach me anymore?"

Qui had to stifle a laugh. "No, Mr. Zhuang, I think you have learned enough already to be able to continue your work here if you so desire."

"Oh, I do, Sir," Zhuang said. "But…" He stopped.

"But, what?" Qui said.

"I am not sure how I should ask, Sir, but…"

Qui said, "Just ask!"

After a pause, Zhuang said, "Was there anything about his work here which caused Mr. Wang's death?"

"No," Qui said. "Not at all."

Zhuang sighed heavily. "That is a relief."

Qui asked, "Do you have any questions for me?"

"Yes, Sir," Zhuang said, "I have helped Mr. Wang haul the pig carcasses to the incinerator, but I do not know where he got the key to the truck."

"You will get the key from my secretary."

Zhuang stood and thanked the lieutenant and left the office.

CHAPTER 3

Chicago, Illinois, USA
January 6, 2020,
8:10 am, Central Standard Time

Chinese graduate student Li Song Wi loaded two suitcases into the trunk of his yellow Nissan Sentra. Inside the car he stowed a roll of graded papers in the glove box. He drove to Benjamin Franklin Technical University, moved the roll of papers to his overcoat pocket and entered the chemistry department. There he found Professor Thaddeus Halsworth in his office.

"Good morning, Li," the professor said gladly. "Do you have the papers from my 101 class done yet? I'd like to look them over before I pass them out today."

Li pulled the rolled-up papers from his pocket. "Yes, Sir, they are right here." Li handed the roll to the professor who removed the rubber band holding them and lay them on his desk.

"The students did very well on this test, Sir." Li watched as the professor unfolded the papers and saw the stack of U. S. one-hundred-dollar bills inside.

As Halsworth opened his side desk drawer and scooped the money inside, he removed another roll of papers from the same drawer. He closed and locked the drawer and slid the new roll of papers across to Li. "Here is your next stack of papers to be graded. How soon can you have them graded?"

Li answered, "I believe I can return them by Friday."

"Great, then I will see you Friday morning." Li smiled. He

knew it would be three days before Halsworth knew Li was gone. By that time, he would be home in China, in time to see the birth of his first child, a boy.

Li peered into the roll of papers and saw they and a brown envelope were wrapped around the glass vial of viscous purple liquid. He smiled and left the office. This was the last exchange he would be required to make with Professor Thaddeus Halsworth. Others from his division would continue contact with the professor, but, for now, his part was done. Li despised Halsworth. The information China gained from Halsworth was valuable and would help the Chinese catch up with America's bio/germ warfare arsenal, but Li hated him because Halsworth was a traitor to his own country. A man who would betray his country for money was the worst kind of scum Li could imagine.

Li walked to his car and drove out of the parking lot. He did not notice the black van leaving the lot across the street at the same time. He drove to Interstate 94 then turned south. He followed I-94 south at a steady speed then turned northwest on I-90. He followed I-90 and entered O'Hare International Airport. The black van was four cars behind him. When a red and white Chevrolet pickup pulled in between them, the van turned off into a cell phone lot. Li drove to the Delta Terminal where he parked the yellow Nissan in a short-term lot, removed the two suitcases from his trunk and went inside. At the ticket desk, he gave the ticket agent his passport identifying him as Li Song Wi and used a prepaid Mastercard to pay US $2,509.00 for a one-way ticket to Wuhan, China.

He checked both suitcases into baggage and placed his boarding pass, ticket, and baggage check stubs in his inside coat pocket. On the way to his gate, he stopped at a newsstand, bought a local newspaper, a bottle of orange juice, a cookie, and a small bottle of mouthwash. He sat at a small table in the common area. He drew his cell phone from his shirt pocket and pressed a single button. The person he was calling did not answer and, when the voice mail began the welcome message, he disconnected.

As he took a sip of juice, the man on the walkway above the clock snapped a picture with a telephoto lens. Every few seconds he snapped another. After three minutes, a man with an overnight bag and a cup of steaming coffee approached Li. "Looks like every table is taken. Do you mind if I sit down?"

Li stared at him blankly. He used this ploy often to make westerners think he spoke no English and usually they would leave.

When Li did not answer, the man repeated his question. In perfect Mandarin. Li was shocked. There were not many round-eyes who could speak Mandarin with no accent and with perfect grammar. Li motioned for the man to sit, and he did so. The man introduced himself as Christopher Weber, an accountant from Houston. He told Li he had been in Chicago for a week conducting an audit and was headed home for a couple of days rest, then on to their new office in Beijing.

Weber leaned closer across the little table and said, "I'll make you a deal, Mr. Whatever your name really is. If you promise not to run, I will promise not to put a bullet in the back of your pointy little Chinese skull. How does that strike you?" Weber opened the lapel of his coat, and Li saw the 9 mm in Weber's shoulder holster. "Oh, hell, I'm not really an accountant, I work for the FBI and you are under arrest, China Boy."

Li looked to his right and saw two more men who were

probably FBI; to his left, two more. A man grabbed Li roughly from behind and pushed his face down hard against the tabletop. As Li was being cuffed, Weber said, "Listen to this, China Boy, you have the right to remain silent…" and read the full Miranda warning to him, again in perfect Mandarin. When he finished, he told Li it was just a formality. "You see, China Boy, you are under arrest for espionage, and we are not charging you with a U. S. Code violation. We are charging you with espionage under the Patriot Act. That means you get no lawyer, no bond, no rights, no embassy contact and no visitors. We will take you to a secure location where you will be interrogated by whatever means we so desire, and there is nothing you can do to stop it." Weber was lying, but he was betting Li was not familiar with the Patriot Act. "This would be the appropriate time for you to be so scared you piss your pants." Weber stepped back and looked at Li's pants. "No pee, Guys. I guess we've got us a hard case here. Search him closely. Look in his mouth, his ears, his nose and his asshole. Make sure he has no suicide pill. He can't talk if he's dead."

While the other agents started searching Li, Weber picked up Li's travel bag. He saw the rolled-up papers and pulled the rubber band off exposing the glass vial and the brown envelope. He reached into his coat pocket and removed a pair of Nitrile Latex Gloves. He removed the glass vial and held it up for the others to see. "Who's documenting today?"

"That's me, Chris," another agent said.

Chris said, "Come take a look. I don't know what this is but this stopper in the end of the vial looks mighty secure. I found it in this bag. Take a picture when I put it back in. It was wrapped up in these papers and secured with this rubber band." When the photos were finished, Chris opened the brown envelope wrapped around the vial. Inside he saw a drafting diagram of part of a building. Take a picture of this, Greg. What does this look like to you?"

Greg took a picture of the drawing and then examined it. "Some kind of chemical set up, Chris. Hey, I know who can tell us." He looked around until he saw the agent he was looking for. "Hey Ed, come look at this. What was your major in college, Ed?"

"Chemistry," said Ed. "Why?"

"Look at this and tell us what it is." He handed the drawing to Ed then wrote Ed's name on his evidence contact list, indicating everyone who had touched the drawing in case it was fingerprinted later.

"This looks like a portion of a chemical processing facility. See this double line? You can follow it all the way through. It's the carrier…like a conveyor…that carries the substance through the process."

"What kind of material would something like this process?" Chris asked.

Ed paused. "I can't be sure without seeing the completed diagram, but I'm about ninety percent sure this is part of a set up for processing organic material into weaponized material."

"Okay," Chris said, "say that in English for us non-chemistry majors."

"With this set up, a mediocre chemist could make a *helluva* dirty bomb. A good chemist could make a *lot* of dirty bombs, if he had the right material," Ed said.

Chris said, "What color would the bad stuff be?"

"It varies," Ed answered. "It just depends on what the base material was."

"Okay, Ed," Chris said. "What would the stuff look like?"

Ed was silent a moment then said, "It would probably be a thick, viscous liquid. If it were green, we would know it came from plant matter. Brown would be from pig poop."

"Don't mess with me, Ed." Chris said.

Ed continued, acting like he never heard a word Chris said. He mentioned a few other colors like yellow and pink then said, "The worst, the most unstable and most dangerous would be purple. If you find a vial of purple viscous liquid, run away. Run away very fast. A test tube of the purple stuff can eliminate half of Chicago in a week. It won't explode, but it can pass from human to human in a New York minute!

"Chris stuck his hand into the travel bag and removed the vial. "Would it be about this shade of purple, Ed?"

Ed took three quick steps backward, pulled out his handkerchief and used it to cover his mouth and nose. "Jesus H. Christ, Chris. You are one crazy S. O. B. Everyone move back!" he shouted. "Stay away from Chris. Chris, you and Greg may have been exposed, you will have to be quarantined until we get you tested." Ed pulled out his cell phone and pushed one button. When someone answered, he said, "This is Ed Martin, ID 546. I have a level three Biohazard Exposure Incident, O'Hare Airport, Delta terminal, food court. Ed looked around the group counting noses. "There are five Class A, two Class B, one X-Ray and about fifty passengers who were nearby."

Ed listened for a moment then said, "546 standing by. How long?" He listened for a moment. "Not good enough. I need them faster. Chopper them in NOW! Either do it or let me talk to the general". He paused again. "Don't bullshit me. I have his number programmed into my phone, but you and I both know he's standing right next to you listening to our conversation. Now get me those choppers in here and make sure they have hazmat gear. Three of them." He listened for another moment. "I am going to have three choppers here in fifteen minutes, or I will call a friend who will gladly send choppers with hazmat gear and occupied by people who have no idea what you mean when you say, "Do not say ANYTHING to the press and DO NOT SELL YOUR STORY TO THE NATIONAL ENQUIRER."

CHAPTER 4

Chicago, Illinois, USA
January 26, 2020
8:40 am, Central Standard Time

Another Chinese student, Jin Lu Sohn was pulling into the Chemistry building parking lot while Li was pulling out. He turned around to follow Li. Jin wanted to talk to him about the transfer when he saw the black van following Li. Jin wanted to call him to let him know he was being followed but had left his cell phone at home. As they entered the airport, the black van turned into a cell phone lot just as a red and white pick-up entered the lane behind Li. Li parked in the short-term parking as did the pick-up. Jin continued to the regular parking and went inside.

After ten minutes of searching, Jin saw Li sitting at a small table in the food court area. When he started walking toward the glass wall that separated him from Li inside the security area, a man in a black coat approached and spoke to Li. After he spoke, the man sat down. Jin watched as five other men gathered around Li and one of them slammed Li's head to the table and began putting handcuffs on his wrists.

Jin turned and walked back to his car. He drove quickly to his house to destroy documents and clear out his personal belongings. He parked in the alley behind the house and entered through the kitchen. Just as he opened the door, three men grabbed him and pushed him to the floor. One of them put a handgun to the back of his head. "I am from the FBI and you are under arrest for espionage under the Patriot Act. We also have a warrant to search your house. Just lay there until we are ready to talk to you."

Jin watched as they searched and hoped they would not find the hidden room he built beside the large bedroom. Jin saw flashes from cameras and saw the light of the video recorder. One of the men stood over Jin with his foot planted heavily on Jin's back. When Jin tried to move, the man put his weight on that foot.

"Hey, Tim, come look at this." Agent Tim Bellow walked into the bedroom in response to the other agent's call.

"What's up?" Tim asked.

"Does this room look odd to you?" Jin closed his eyes tightly.

Tim looked around the room and said, "Hey, it looks kind of lopsided now that you mention it. But why?"

The agent said, "There's fresh paint drops on the floor in front of this wall, like it was recently painted."

"Or," Tim said, "recently built."

"I think that's it, Tim. I think we've got a fake wall here with a room hidden behind it."

Tim walked back to the living room and squatted down in front of Jin. "Where's the entrance to your secret room?"

Jin said nothing.

Tim asked again. "How do you get into the secret room?"

Again, Jin said nothing.

Tim said, "Andy, go to the van and get the battering ram and a couple of pry bars." Another agent trotted out the door. He returned in thirty seconds carrying the two-man battering ram and two pry bars. Tim said, "Lend a hand, guys. Make a doorway in that wall."

Four agents began banging, prying, and punching until they made a hole four feet tall and two-and-a-half feet wide. A light shone through all the dust like sunbeams through a forest fog. "That's enough", Tim said. He bent and walked through the hole and into a room four feet deep and twelve feet wide. As Tim took a step, he heard an electronic beep. He never heard anything else. The entire house exploded with the force of four pounds of C-4 which had been set to blow the house if the alarm had not been reset by the entrance through the floor from the basement. Everyone in the house and the two adjacent houses died that day, including Jin.

CHAPTER 5

Chicago, Illinois, USA
January 6, 2020
9:12 am, Central Standard Time

The explosion near the campus shook the office of Professor Thaddeus Halsworth. He walked to the window and saw the smoke rising from the old neighborhood two blocks from the campus. The neighborhood was populated by many students who took chemistry so they would have access to equipment and supplies to cook meth. He wondered if it was any of his students who had made a mistake when cooking the stuff. He locked his office door and, as he counted the money from his desk drawer, he heard the wail of sirens as firetrucks, cop cars and ambulances reverberated between the tall brick buildings of the campus.

As Halsworth counted, rookie FBI agent Sandra Hellis screamed into her radio, "I need help now, damnit. They were all inside and now the house is gone."

"The woman on the other end of the radio said, "Calm down, what do you mean 'the house is gone?' How can you lose a house?"

"I didn't lose it, asshole. It exploded. I need fire, ambulance, police and an FBI supervisor and a bomb team. Get on it."

Limping badly, Hellis made her way through the smoke and haze. Even though she was in great pain, she tried to reach blindly through the smoke to open the door but discovered there was no door left. She sat on the low brick wall by the porch and cried. She looked at her torn pants and saw part of her broken femur sticking up through her ripped skin. She remembered her car being flipped by the explosion and landing on her, trapping one leg under it. Now she realized her leg was hurting.

At the airport, the agents were walking to the parking lot with Li in tow when Chris' cell phone rang. "Weber," he barked. He listened for a moment. "Say that again." Another pause. "Oh, God." He quit walking. "I'm going there now. I'll have some of my team members bring China Boy in and I'll…" He was interrupted. "But, SAC, those were my friends." Another pause. "Yes, Sir. Yes, Sir. I understand and I will be there shortly. Who are you sending? That's good. He's a good man. Knows what he's doing. I will see you in about an hour." He stuffed his cell phone in his pocket and continued walking toward his truck. "Ed, put this turd in the van and let's get going." After Li was secured in the van and out of earshot, Ed asked, "What's wrong, Chris?"

"Tim's team was searching Jin's house and there was an explosion which took out the house and the houses on either side."

"And the team?" Ed asked.

"All gone. Everyone except the rookie. She was on watch outside. She's en route to the hospital. Her car was flipped and landed on her leg."

Another agent asked, "Are we going?"

"No," Chris said. "SAC is sending Tommy's team."

"Crap," Ed said. "Why not us?"

"SAC wants us to get started interrogating Li right away. We have orders. Let's move. Ed, you ride with me," Chris said. As he pulled out of the airport, Chris said, "Okay, Ed, who is the general? And what was all that about on the phone?"

Ed said, "First of all, Chris, I have a question I need to ask you."

"Okay, shoot," Chris said.

"I heard you call the suspect Li 'China Boy' several times."

Chris said, "So?"

Ed continued. "Chris, do you have some kind of hatred for Chinese people or other Asians?"

"No," Chris said. "It was just a matter of convenience for me."

"Convenience?" Ed asked. "What do you mean convenience?"

Chris said, "I got so excited about catching this guy after such a long investigation…" he paused," that I forgot his damn name, okay? Call it 'stupid' on my part. Why are you asking me about this? Has there been a complaint made against me?"

"No," Ed said. "I just needed to make sure you are not predisposed to have negative feelings toward Chinese people before I answered your question about the general. Chris, what I'm about to tell you is top secret. I can read you in, but you cannot include anyone below your grade. Do you understand that?"

"I do."

From a briefcase, Ed produced an FBI form which would acknowledge Ed had informed Chris that the information he was about to impart was top secret. Chris reviewed and signed the document while driving.

Ed continued, "Chris, for the last two years I have been assigned to a special task force called 'Mongoose'. We have been tracking some Chinese agents who have been trying to find a way into our country's chemical and biological warfare section. The guy in the van who calls himself Li Song Wi is really a lieutenant in the Chinese Army named Qui Din Wa."

"Din Wa?" Chris asked. "Like the Chinese restaurant on Strickland Drive?"

"Almost, except for the fact the restaurant is called Din How, Wa really is his name, not How, and Wa is assigned to a secret lab hidden inside the University of Wuhan, China. It's in the Hubei Province on the Yangtze River about eleven hundred and fifty kilometers south of Beijing. The locals call it the 'University in the Trees' and the heavy forests around and inside the university make it hard for our satellites to see anything through the canopy of trees. We can still see some stuff, especially with FLIR (Forward Looking InfraRed), but not a lot.

"Three years ago, we had human intel inside the university who alerted us to the fact that a secret lab was being built in the basement of a new chemistry building. We lost contact with our guy. Two years ago, we moved part of our bio/chem weapons program to the Chemistry department of Benjamin Franklin University here in Chicago. We thought we were safe because the process for making the samples, the fuel of the program, was being conducted in Maryland and the process for converting it was being done here by a professor who created the process.

"Then, about eighteen months ago, a Chinese professor defected through India and knocked on the door of the U. S. embassy in Delhi and asked for asylum. His name was Li Song Wi. Li was on our list of friendlies and may have been the CIA's man in Wuhan. The agency got him hired as a 'graduate student' in the chemistry department at BFU. Soon, U. S. secrets started showing up in Wuhan at the university. We put Li under surveillance in a joint venture with the FBI, CIA and the Army. The CIA handled the work in China, we handled the work in the U. S. and the Army filled in with support and logistics as needed.

"The Chinese needed the purple liquid you found in Li's travel bag, and they also needed the plans to build their lab to operate exactly like ours. We believe the drawing you found in the bag is the final part of the laboratory plan to complete the process. If the Chinese get their hands on those two things, we are in deep doo-doo.

"Jesus H. Christ," Chris said. "So, who is this general guy you talked about on the phone?"

"The general is General Nobody. No one knows his name, no one tells his name. Everyone just calls him 'The General'. I'm not sure he's even a general, but I do know he oversees all of this. I take my orders directly from him. The FBI keeps me on the payroll to hide me from the Chinese. Whenever I am needed, I just take sick leave or vacation, but it never gets on the books. I still have all my sick leave, family leave and vacation time accrued."

Chris pulled to the side of the road and skid to a stop in a gravel parking lot. He slammed the gear-shift lever into 'Park', turned toward Ed and said, "Wait a minute. So, you're telling me Agnes doesn't really have cancer?"

"Oh, hell no, Chris. My wife is as healthy as a horse. She agreed to play along without knowing what I was doing. She trusts me. That's why we haven't seen anyone socially in over a year. By this time people would expect her to look emaciated and hollow-eyed. Hell, she looks better than I do."

"She didn't even share this with my wife?" Chris asked. "She's her own sister, for Christ's sake!"

Ed said, "And Agnes is constantly having to create new excuses to avoid seeing Susan in person."

"So, you mean Agnes is intentionally keeping Susan in the

dark?"

"Sorry, Chris. She wasn't allowed to tell her. And neither are you," Ed said.

"Oh, hold on a minute, Ed. I don't keep things from my…"

Ed interrupted. "You'll keep **this** from her, Chris. I told you this was top secret and now that I've read you into it, you may never tell her. When it's all over, the plan is for Agnes to suddenly go into remission and have a spiritually induced miracle healing and, in time, she will be completely healthy again. Chris, she is doing this for her country for free, and I am asking you to go along with the plan."

"Well, crap," Chris said. "Okay, but she better not really get sick or anything." He was silent for a moment. "Wait a minute. If this purple liquid is so damn dangerous, why did the guys in the hazmat suits just give it back to you and not quarantine you and Greg and me?"

Ed said, "They tested it, a simple test on site, and discovered it was the base material and had not been weaponized yet."

"What does that mean, Ed? Weaponized?"

"It means it has not yet undergone the process which changes it from an inert material into a highly volatile and dangerous substance."

CHAPTER 6

FBI Headquarters
Chicago, Illinois, USA
January 6, 2020
10:15 am, Central Standard Time

When Chris and Ed arrived at the main Chicago office, the team members were placing Qui into an interview room with a black cloth bag over his head. The Special Agent in Charge (SAC), of the Chicago field office, Harvey Walker, referred to by his subordinates as "SAC", came to Chris' office. "You okay, Chris?"

"Hell, no," he said. "I'm not okay, SAC. We just lost a whole team of agents. People I worked with, people who have been to my house. I just want to walk into that room and shoot that Chinese bastard in the head, but that would be counter-productive, now wouldn't it, Boss?

SAC laughed. "Your language really does slay me sometimes, Chris. However, I do understand what you mean. Ed," SAC said, "did you read Chris into your assignment?"

"I did, SAC," Ed said.

"Do you need him?"

"We do, SAC."

"Okay. Chris, until you are no longer needed you will work with Ed on whatever it is he is working on. I don't know what it is, I don't want to know what it is. Ed is a senior investigator, the most senior special agent in the Chicago office and works well without direct supervision. Also, yesterday the Director of the

CIA called the Director of the FBI who called the Attorney General in Washington who unexpectedly sat down at my table at Starbuck's this morning here in Chicago and bought me some coffee and a roll. He said Ed was deeply involved in something called 'Mongoose' which the AG knew nothing about and because our investigation of this biologic/chem weapons technology has now intersected 'Mongoose', the CIA would like to have Chris assigned to that program for the time being, and the President was going to move some funds around so I could replace you for the time being.

"Later, POTUS called me personally and thanked me and said he had already caused the funds to be moved and, he said, after doing some checking on assistant SAC Christopher Weber of the Chicago office, he decided one man would not be sufficient to carry the load so he's giving us two slots. Who is it in Mongoose who's got so much stroke, Ed?"

Before Ed could speak, SAC said, "Never mind. I don't think I would feel safe knowing that."

Chris asked, "So you know what is going on in this Mongoose program?"

As he stood to leave, SAC said, "No, and I don't want to know. I don't want anyone to tell me anything someone else might torture me to learn about someday. Just pretend you're still working for me and be seen around the office occasionally." He left the office.

An agent knocked, then entered Chris' office without waiting to be told. He placed a cardboard box in the middle of the desk and said, "This is everything China Boy had on him." The agent then left the room. Chris and Ed stood at the desk and began to examine the contents of the box. Ed removed a wallet and began looking through it. He removed a folded paper and showed it to Chris. It was a label for Scope's new grape flavor mouthwash.

Chris said, "I didn't know Scope had a grape flavor."

Ed said, "They don't. I'll bet this is a fake label Qui had so he could get the purple poison on the plane."

"That makes perfect sense to me," Chris said.

Ed removed another folded paper from the wallet. When he unfolded it a round white pill fell onto the table. "Gee," he said, "I wonder what that's for. Can you spell suicide? Why didn't he keep it handy and try to use it?"

Chris said, "No idea. Probably thought he wouldn't need it. Are we going to get started interviewing Qui?"

"No," Ed said. "We've got a guy coming in later this afternoon to do that."

"Coming from where?" Chris asked.

"China," said Ed. "Wuhan, China."

"Who the hell is going to come here from Wuhan to interview a Chinese spy from Wuhan?"

"Bobby Spencer. He's our guy now working in the secret lab under the chemistry building at the University of Wuhan. He left China yesterday when you decided we would take down Qui today. He'll be here about four."

"Does he have some kind of special interrogation talent or something?"

"Or something," Ed said. Both men continued going through the box.

At 4:01 pm, the intercom light on Chris' phone lit up. He answered, "Weber." There was a pause and Chris said, "Yeah, he's right here." He handed the phone to Ed.

"Ed Martin." Pause. "That would be me." Pause. "Thanks,

would you please have him escorted to Weber's office? Thanks. What? He's wearing a what? That's okay."

In three minutes, a clerk knocked on the office door and Chris said, "Enter!" The clerk opened the door and escorted in a man wearing jeans, a t-shirt and a black ski mask then left.

Both men stood and Ed stuck out his hand. "Bobby?" he asked.

The man closed the door behind him, removed the mask and shook Ed's hand. Bobby Spencer was a Chinese man with a scruffy beard and unkempt hair. He shook Chris' hand and asked, "You the guy who speaks Mandarin?"

"That's right. Chris Weber. Why do you look so familiar, Bobby?"

Bobby said, "West Point, class of 2011. You kept me walking punishment tours for a month. Then, when I graduated, they sent me to your unit in Kandahar, I think just to piss you off. I regretted not getting to know you better at the point, but second year cadets don't have many opportunities to mingle with fourth year cadets."

"Ahh, I remember you now. You had the absolute worst attitude toward upper classmen of any cadet in the history of the Point. You seemed to enjoy going out of your way to be rude to them. I overheard you make wise ass comments to them or about them repeatedly."

"But not to you, Chris. Only to the ones who were rude or talked down to me because my eyes weren't round. Or who thought they were smarter than me because they got there two years before me. Those I couldn't stand," Bobby said.

How did you get involved in all this Mongoose business?" Chris asked.

Bobby said, "After Afghanistan I was sent to language school. Since my family spoke several dialects of Chinese, I was tapped to help on that front. When we needed someone on the ground in Wuhan, I drew the short straw." He turned to Ed. "Has Chris been read in, Ed?"

"He has," Ed replied.

"So, I was able to get to the University in Wuhan posing as a peasant looking for low level manual labor. One thing led to another and I got hired as sort of an assistant janitor. It gives me great access and I keep my eyes and ears open and my mouth shut. I found out Qui's real name and job and forwarded the info to the general. I've also learned they are about to complete the production part of the lab. They're just waiting for one more set of drawings and the sample to be processed, but I can't find out who is sending it. I understand you guys screwed up that deal for them."

"That we did," Chris said. "We've got Qui cooling his heels in an interview room, cuffed and wearing a black hood. When do you want to start on him?"

Bobby said, "How about right now?"

"Works for me," Chris said. As the three men prepared to leave the office, Bobby replaced the black ski mask and followed the other two down a long hall to the interrogation room. Chris and Ed entered the next room where they could see and hear everything through a two-way mirror.

Bobby entered the room where the prisoner sat, chained to the desk. He jerked the black hood from Qui's head and said, in Mandarin, "Let's talk." Chris translated for Ed as the conversation continued.

Chris said, "Bobby just told him we want the name of the person who has been giving them the drawings and the biologic samples." Qui said nothing. "Now he's telling Qui things would go better for him if he cooperated with us." Still, Qui said nothing. As Bobby continued to talk to Qui, Chris continued to tell Ed what was being said.

"Now Bobby's telling him that it would be unfortunate if innocent lives were ruined because he refused to cooperate." Bobby reached into an inside coat pocket and, one by one, laid a series of photographs on the desk in front of Qui. Qui looked at the photos of a house, his another house and a beautiful Chinese woman who looked extremely pregnant. Chris said, "Oh, crap. Bobby just told him we know who his wife is and where she lives. He said it would be simply horrible if three or four of our guys were to rape his wife and cut her baby out of her while she is still alive then kill the baby. Jesus, Ed, this guy is vicious."

Ed replied, "Only as vicious as he needs to be."

Qui began straining at his cuffs which were secured to a metal ring atop the table. He began stammering and spitting and talking so fast Chris had trouble understanding him.

Chris said, "Well, it appears Qui's loyalty to his wife outweighs his loyalty to his country. Professor Thaddeus Halsworth is our traitor." By the time Bobby Spenser left the interrogation room, Qui was sobbing. Chris watched through the two-way mirror as Qui's shoulders undulated with each rasping breath and wail. Ed and Chris met Bobby in the hallway.

Chris said, "Man, you are one hard assed meanie."

Bobby said, "The saddest part of all this is his wife died two days ago giving birth. The baby didn't survive, either."

Ed said, "I'll bet if he ever gets home and finds out, he is gonna really be pissed."

Chris said, "I suspect he is never going home. Not alive, anyway."

CHAPTER 7

FBI Headquarters
Chicago, Illinois, USA
January 6, 2020
5:49 an, Central Standard Time

Back in Chris' office, Ed asked, "Bobby, why do you think Qui caved in so easily?"

Bobby said, "I think his supervisors had no idea how much he loved his wife and their unborn son. He was from a prestigious communist party family with a dad who was a general in the People's Liberation Army and a mom who was a university medical professor. He got his position based partly on what he was and partly on who he was. Someone missed something somewhere on his screening. His wife's father is a member of the politburo and her mother is a doctor in Beijing. You couldn't ask for better credentials."

Chris asked, "Are heads gonna roll over this? Back in China, I mean."

"Probably," Bobby said. "But not until they find out what happened to him. As far as they know now, he is just MIA. We are already circulating the story through some third-world allies that he was killed in the same explosion which took out his partner and his partner's house."

Chris said, "So how did you get away from China on such short notice to be here today, Bobby?"

"That's easy," Bobby said. "Bobby is here in Chicago, but

Zhuang Wei is visiting his sick grandmother in Zhaopan, a city northwest of Wuhan. If the university tries to verify it, the local magistrate will confirm it along with a sighting of Zhuang in Zhaopan just this morning."

"Which morning?"

"Whichever morning the inquiry is made," Bobby said.

Ed asked, "So what is the agency's plan of attack from here?"

Bobby answered, "I have requested ten micro-processing devices which will allow us to bug the offices and labs in the science building at the university. Plus, since I am now the new head janitor there, I can move freely about the offices at night to snoop. Also, I have recently discovered a plot by several of the Chinese nationals working for our friends in the Kremlin. They are still trying to figure out what research is being done there. I think I shall inadvertently find a Russian made listening device in one of the labs and report it to the Colonel in charge. If anything is discovered now, it should look like the Russians did it and not us."

"When are you headed back?" Ed asked.

"I'm booked on a midnight flight out of O'Hare with a stop in L.A. then a change in Beijing to Wuhan. I should arrive there about six a.m. local time and be able to change clothes and get some sleep before I go to work at the university at four local time.

"In the meantime, I'm going to zip by the house, say hello to the wife and kids and eat some real homestyle cooking for a change before I head for the airport."

Ed asked, "What do you consider 'homestyle cooking', Bobby? Chop suey?"

"God no, Ed. I grew up in Georgia. So did my wife. We're having liver and onions with corn bread," Bobby said. To Chris, he said, "Are you headed west by any chance, Chris?"

Chris answered, "I am. You need a ride?"

"I sure do," he said. "How long before you're ready?"

Chris answered, "How about right now?"

Before any of them could move toward the door, Chris' phone rang. He picked up the receiver and said, "Weber." He listened for a moment then said, "We were just about to leave but we'll stop by there before we go." He hung up the phone. He said t both men. "That was Martha. She's got the video from Oscar's buttonhole camera ready. She says it has a good image but it's nobody she knows. She wants us all to stop by on the way out to look at it. In five minutes, all three men were in the tech's lab looking at the grainy image of a very ugly Chinese woman using a linoleum knife to cut Oscar's throat followed by a torrent of blood covering the tiny lens.

Martha asked, "Do any of you gentlemen recognize that pretty little lady?" No one did. "Well," she said, "that video is like a fingerprint. It does us no good if we don't have something to compare it with."

Bobby asked, "Martha, can you run that image through the department's facial recognition software? Maybe you can get something there."

Martha answered, "I can try. I can't guarantee anything, and it will probably take a while."

Chris said, "Great, you weren't planning on doing anything tonight, were you?"

Martha said, "I had considered sleeping for an hour or two, possibly even three."

"Great," Chris said. "We're all going home to spend some time with our families. You stay here and work. Remember, I still owe you a steak dinner."

As the three men left the lab, Martha kicked off her shoes, turned to her computer and said over her shoulder, "You're still an asshole, Weber."

Chris stopped suddenly and turned to Martha. "Listen, while you're playing around in here with all your little electronic gadgets, see if you can find me a good image of a Chinese infant, maybe three to five days old. I need one that looks like it was taken with a cell phone camera. Make sure there are no identifying marks like a blanket or any furniture. Print it and have it for me first thing in the morning. Thanks, you're a trooper."

Martha answered, "And you're still an asshole."

In the car, Bobby asked, "Do you have something special planned for a photo of a Chinese infant, Chris?"

"I'm hoping to convince Qui it's a photo of his son in case I need to squeeze him a bit. I may tell him his wife is dead, but his son is still alive and in our hands. It may build a fire under him to tell us more about what we need to know. That baby may save to world from doom for all we know."

Bobby said, "Wow. Now who's the hard ass meanie?"

Twenty minutes after later, Chris arrived home. Walking in the front door, he was immediately attacked by three ninja-type assassins. The four-year-old boy grabbed one leg and the three and two-year-old girls shared the other. Chris' wife Lisa did not hear the door open then close; she only heard the children's screams of glee which she interpreted as fear. She ran into the foyer with a spatula in her hand just in time to see Chris slide down the wall into a heap on the floor. She playfully knelt on the floor next to the writhing pile of bodies and joined the melee.

"Welcome home, G-man," she said. "You're late. What are you working on so hard lately that makes you late most nights?"

"Oh, you know," he said. "Big important ASAC stuff. Lots of paperwork and reports and meetings and such. Keeping America safe."

They all stood and walked into the kitchen, except for the two-year-old who rode her daddy's foot into the kitchen. "What is that smell?" he asked.

"It's what's for supper," she said. "Liver and onions."

"You're kidding," he said.

CHAPTER 8

Wuhan, Hubei District, China
January 8, 2020
3:55 pm, China Standard Time

When a bleary-eyed Zhuang Wei stumbled out of his shed just before four in the afternoon, he stumbled to his overturned waste basket with a cup of tea. He had been seated only a moment when Lieutenant Ming, Qui's replacement, came outside and sat next to him on another wastebasket. Zhuang started to stand, but the lieutenant motioned for him to remain seated. "How is your grandmother, Zhuang?" he said.

"She is much better. With the money I earn here I was able to buy medicines for her and she is improving. I am lucky to have such a good job here. I cannot thank the university enough for allowing me to continue working here."

"I must warn you," the lieutenant said, "while you have been away, there has been a concerning new development in Wuhan. Did the doctors tell you what manner of ailment your grandmother suffered?"

"Not exactly," Zhuang said. "I think he said it was a stomach flu."

"Are you sure he did not say it was a respiratory illness?"

"No, Sir," Zhuang said. "He said her lungs were clear and it was a good thing since many elderly people suffer from pneumonia when they are ill with other maladies."

"Maladies?" the lieutenant asked.

"I do not really know what it means. It is a word the doctor used at home," Zhuang said. "Why do you ask?"

The lieutenant said, "While you were away, an influenza epidemic broke out here in Wuhan and has taken the lives of twelve people and three times that many are sick."

"How did this start?" Zhuang asked.

"We do not know how it started," the lieutenant said, "but we know where it started."

"Where?"

"In the central market area on the street of the meat cutters," he said.

Zhuang immediately thought of the pigs Wang sold to his brother, the meat cutter. "Did someone sell some bad meat?"

"We don't know yet. The local police are investigating. They are interviewing the families of the dead to find out if they have any visits or purchases in common."

Zhuang asked, "What does that mean?"

"It means the police want to know if any of the sick or dead people shopped at the same place in the market area."

"I do hope they find the source soon," Bobby said. "And no one else is made sick."

The lieutenant stood to go. "As do I, Zhuang. As do I."

As the lieutenant walked away, Bobby made the decision he had to say something. "Lieutenant?"

The lieutenant turned and stood, silent.

Bobby said, "I do not know if this is important or not, but…"

"What?" the lieutenant asked.

"Were you aware Mr. Weng was tasked with taking three pigs to the incinerator every Friday?" Zhuang asked.

"I was not aware of this," the lieutenant said.

"Then, when Mr. Weng died, I was tasked with doing the same. Once when we worked together, Mr. Weng told me we were not going to take the pigs to the incinerator but would take them to his brother's meat market in the city market area to sell. His brother gave Weng some money for the pigs and Weng split the money with me."

The lieutenant's face turned ashen.

"Could this have anything to do with the illness which is happening now?" Bobby asked.

"Come with me, now!" the lieutenant said. He marched back into the building and down to the basement. He led Zhuang to an unmarked door where he knocked and entered without waiting for a reply. He quickly motioned for Zhuang to sit and said, "Mr. Zhuang, tell the colonel what you just told me."

Zhuang repeated his story for the colonel, ending with, "Is this something we should not have done?"

"I do not know yet, Mr. Zhuang. I will find out, though. Please wait outside my office."

"Yes, Sir," Zhuang said. "Should I begin my daily cleaning now?"

"No, just sit and wait," the colonel said.

Zhuang sat where the colonel could see him, twisting his hat in his hands in his best peasant imitation. In ten minutes, the colonel called to him. "Mr. Zhuang, come in here."

When Zhuang stood before him, the colonel said, "Mr. Zhuang, do you think you could lead me to this meat market again?"

"I think so, Sir, but I was there only one time."

"We will go to the market area in my car and the local police will meet us there. Will you go with me?"

"I will, Sir. Maybe it means nothing but if it matters, perhaps we can stop this before more people die."

In thirty minutes, the colonel's car pulled up in front of the market of Mr. Weng's brother. The local police swarmed into the store with guns drawn and, when Zhuang entered, he identified one of the men as Mr. Weng's brother, the owner of the market, and two of the other men as the two who had unloaded the pigs from the truck. He did not know the fourth man in the market, a man who looked pale and unsteady. When the man fainted, everyone moved away from him. He began shaking and foam came from his mouth before he became rigid and died.

It was after nine before Zhuang and the two military men returned to the university. The colonel said to Zhuang, "The local police want to talk to you more tomorrow. I told them they could reach you here through the lieutenant. You did very well in telling me about this. Why don't you take the rest of the night off?

"Sir, I cannot do that. I have done none of my cleaning today. I must clean the labs and classrooms and empty all the wastebaskets and the shredder boxes before I can end my day," Zhuang said.

"I suppose you are right, Mr. Zhuang. Go ahead about your daily duties and thank you for a job done well today." Zhuang bowed and backed out of the room. The lieutenant closed the door and sat.

"Did you have any idea Weng was selling the pigs to his brother?" the colonel asked.

"I did not. Do you think Qui might have known?" Ming asked.

"No. If Qui had known he would have stopped it and told me immediately," the colonel said.

The lieutenant asked, "The pigs that are sent to the

incinerator, are these not the pigs which have been infected with the weaponized virus from the United States?"

The colonel answered, "They are. That is why they are sent to be incinerated."

"I wonder," the lieutenant asked, "just how long Weng sent those infected pigs to his brother's market instead of burning them."

The colonel said, "We have only been infecting them less than a year, so we know it was not more than that. Get Doctor Chu down here. If he has left for the day, get him back here. Now."

In less than an hour, Dr. Chu Nie was sitting in the colonel's office with the colonel and the lieutenant. When Colonel Husan told Dr. Chu what Wang had done, Chu gasped.

"Every one of the pigs he was supposed to burn was infected with one or more strains of virus. That is why I told him to stay with the pigs until they were completely incinerated. If his brother butchered and sold the meat of those pigs, everyone who ate that meat could die. And everyone who encountered the meat or a person who touched the meat can die. I believe the meat market may be ground zero for this outbreak."

There was a knock on the office door and Ming rose to open it. Zhuang stood at the door with a small piece of electronic equipment in his hand. "Sir, I hate to bring more misery to your door, but I believe this is very important."

From behind his desk, the colonel asked, "What are you holding, Mr. Zhuang?"

"I do not know, Sir. I dropped my cleaning rag on the floor in the laboratory and when I bent to pick it up, I saw this device attached with tape to the bottom of a table there. There is a red light showing very faintly. I removed the device and brought it straight here." Zhuang handed the device to Ming. "There is writing on it, but I cannot tell what it says. It is not Mandarin."

Ming looked at the device and handed it to the colonel. "It is Cyrillic."

"What is civilic?" Zhuang asked.

"Not civilic," Ming said. "Cyrillic. It means Russian writing."

"Oh," Zhuang answered. "I am so confused."

Husan said, "Speak to no one of this, Mr. Zhuang."

"Yes, Sir. I mean, No, Sir. I mean I will say nothing, Sir."

The colonel said, "Once again, you have done well Mr. Zhuang."

Zhuang said, "I am glad I could be of some small service to our beloved country."

CHAPTER 9

Wuhan, Hubei District, China
January 9, 2020
4:00 pm, China Standard Time

By four o'clock the next afternoon, the local police in Wuhan had interviewed all the merchants on the meat cutters' street and had closed fourteen shops. By midnight, another twelve people were dead. The university was closed, and a curfew was announced for six p.m. each day.

Since the university was closed, this left Zhuang the perfect opportunity to "go home to see his sick grandmother" again. In ten hours, he was in South Korea and in another two he was abord a military plane bound for the United States and in twelve, he landed at O'Hare airport in Chicago. The next day Zhuang Wei's name appeared on a list of the dead in Zhaopan, Hubei Province, China. The list was signed by the local magistrate, Mr. Chung.

Also, the next day, the Chinese government halted all air traffic in and out of Wuhan. All unnecessary businesses were ordered closed and hospitals geared up for a mass influx of cases. By the third day, one hundred thirty-two people were dead, and hospitals were overflowing with new cases of what the government called a corona virus.

By weeks' end, the virus moved across the globe like dominoes falling one after the other. From China to Japan to South Korea to India to Africa. When the virus hit Italy, the hospitals were overwhelmed daily. Hundreds of people died each day throughout the country. Tourism ceased. Italian cruise ships stopped sailing. St. Peter's closed. Milan shut down. Venice was closed.

In the United States, California was hit hard. Cruise ships destined for California ports were denied permission to dock, left to circle in the pacific waiting for clearance to land somewhere, anywhere. American guests aboard a cruise ship in Japan were denied permission to leave the ship until the United States sent two airplanes to get them. When those planes landed in the U.S., those passengers were quarantined at several U. S. military bases for two weeks.

Day after day, across the U. S. new cases of what was now being called Covid-19 sprang up every day. Citizens were advised to wash their hands for twenty seconds, several times a day, clean surfaces regularly and to practice social distancing, staying six feet apart from other people whenever possible. When the virus reached New York City, five hundred to eight hundred people died every day for weeks.

About the time Bobby Spencer landed at O'Hare airport in Chicago, three visitors arrived at the office of Colonel Husan Ling at the university in Wuhan, China. They walked into the colonel's office without knocking. The men were dressed in civilian clothes but had short haircuts, clean shaven faces and excellent posture. Their very being screamed "Secret Police". The MSS, Ministry of State Security, was China's version of the old KGB of Moscow. They were ruthless and extremely secretive. In military circles in China, the standing joke was, if you had a conscience when you joined the MSS, it would be surgically removed as soon as they discovered it.

Husan greeted the men with, "I assume you gentlemen are from the MSS."

The older of the three replied, "Indeed we are, Colonel Husan. Is Lieutenant Ming still in the building?"

"Probably."

"Please ask him to join us here, Colonel," the man said.

Husan lifted the receiver and dialed a two-digit number. "Could you please come to my office immediately?" He replaced the receiver. "Now, Gentlemen, what brings the MSS to our remote city?"

The same man said, "May we please wait for Lieutenant Ming? It is so much easier if we must say things only once."

By the time he finished his sentence, there was a knock and Ming entered without waiting. He stood to attention and said, "Lieutenant Ming reporting as ordered, Sir." Husan had warned Ming on his first day he liked things to operate on an informal and friendly manner, but when visitors were present, all formalities must be observed.

Husan said, "Gentlemen, this is Lieutenant Ming, my second in command. Lieutenant, I will allow these gentlemen to introduce themselves since I do not know their names."

Without rising, the older man said, "My name is also Ming. These two gentlemen are my associates and their names, for the time being, are not important. We are here in response to the colonel's memo about a Mr. Wang who sold pigs to his brother's market which came from your laboratory here. Also, in the same memorandum, there is mention of a Russian-made listening device discovered within the laboratory here. Tell me, Colonel, what is the connection between the dead pigs and the listening device?"

Husan said, "At this time, I know of no connection between the two. However, since you and your companions are sitting in my office discussing the two topics, I will assume there is a credible chance they are connected. Lieutenant Ming?"

"The only connection I can think of is our janitor Mr. Zhuang," Lieutenant Ming said.

"Why do you say that?" the other Ming asked.

The lieutenant said, "Mr. Zhuang was the one who reported to me, and then to the colonel, that our last janitor, Mr. Wang, instead of burning the carcasses of pigs being used for research, took them to his brother, a local butcher and sold them. The local police have determined our recent outbreak of an unclassified virus was started at Mr. Wang's market in the market district.

"On the same day he revealed this to us he also found a listening device attached under a table in our laboratory which is still being built. The device was sent to your headquarters with the colonel's memo. It appears to be a Russian-made device."

The older man said, "Is Mr. Zhuang at work today?"

"Unfortunately," Husan said, "he is not. When the university closed because of the pandemic, Mr. Zhuang went home to his village to help care for his ailing grandmother."

The man asked, "Can you call him or call someone in his village to go to his house and bring him here so we can interview him?"

The lieutenant said, "Unfortunately, Mr. Zhuang is listed among those in his village who have died due to the pandemic. I telephoned the local magistrate to confirm his death but the magistrate, according to his wife, died this morning."

The older man said, "I want to drive to his village and see the body of this man Zhuang and the magistrate, also."

The lieutenant said, "Again, I regret to inform you the bodies of Mr. Zhuang and Mr. Chung, the magistrate, were cremated this morning as per the decree of the head magistrate here in the Hubei District several days ago."

The older man looked back and forth to his two companions. "Colonel Husan, do you see nothing suspicious in all of this?"

"Sir," the colonel said, "I am an army medical administrator, not a secret police agent. I tend to see things in the light of what is happening which affects my job here at this laboratory which really does not even exist. I am trained to certainly pay attention to things which affect state security, but I do not eat and breathe security as you gentlemen must. That is not my priority. My priority is to execute my mandate to complete the testing we are doing here in hopes to bring things to a satisfactory conclusion."

"And did the recent events lead you to any satisfactory conclusions?"

Husan and the lieutenant gave each other sideways glances. The lieutenant said to Mr. Ming, "Sir, if you need anything else from me, I shall be in my office which is the third door on the left down the main hallway." Without waiting for a reply, the lieutenant left the office. The colonel rose, locked the door, and returned to his seat.

"Sir, as required by the official secrets law, I must now ask each of you to show me your defense secret or top-secret clearance cards." All three men handed their cards to Husan. He examined each and returned them. "Gentlemen, our primary focus in this laboratory which does not officially exist, was to find a way to weaponize certain organic compounds which the Americans were using to study feasibility for inclusion in their chemical and germ warfare program. While trying to replicate their compounds, we discovered one of the compounds we were working with became very unstable. We infected three pigs with this virus and discovered it was almost impossible to control. That is the virus which has now killed almost one thousand people across the country. We have not yet found a cure for this virus. This type of virus is called a corona virus and it is extremely virulent. My previous number two-man, Lieutenant Qui, worked closely with the researchers but he was transferred to another assignment shortly before the virus spread."

Ming said, "Is it Lieutenant Qui Din How?"

"It is," said Husan. "Do you know him?"

Ming said, "May I now see *your* defense secret clearance card, Colonel?"

After Ming had examined the colonel's card, he said, "Qui was transferred to my command when he left here. He was sent to replace a missing scientist and 'escaped' by traveling to Delhi where he showed up at the Embassy of the United States seeking asylum. Once he was accepted as Dr. Li Song Wi, he was sent to a university in Chicago in America where he posed as a graduate student while being our contact with a traitor at the university."

Husan said, "I am glad to hear he is fine."

"No one said he was fine, Colonel. Lieutenant Qui is missing. We have been informed by a source in a friendly European location Qui was in the house of his partner, a man known as Jin Lu Sohn, when the house exploded while being searched by the Federal Bureau of Investigation near the university in Chicago. We suspect Jin rigged his house to explode if anyone besides himself or Qui came in. Apparently, Qui and Jin were both in the house and that house and the two on either side were destroyed. The FBI, so far, has only found body parts and are attempting to match those parts to other parts through DNA.

Husan said, "Oh, what sorrow for his family."

"Why do you say that, Colonel?"

"Because Qui's wife stayed here instead of going to Beijing to have her baby. Unfortunately, there was a sepsis problem and neither Qui's wife nor their child survived. Knowing Qui and his loyalty to his family, I believe, if he were still alive, he would find a way to get back here for his wife and son.

"Mr. Ming, I have been working on a plan in my head which I have not yet converted to writing which may bring about some good to compensate our nation for its recent loss of so many citizens."

"What plan?" Ming asked.

"Have you seen the reports of the devastating effects here in our province from this virus?"

"I have," Ming said.

"Our nation has been hurt, even somewhat crippled by the trade sanctions the new American president has imposed upon China. Our businesses, especially the small, family owned businesses, are being crippled by the loss of revenue caused by these sanctions."

Ming said, "Colonel, business is not my forte. My job is security."

"But those things go hand in hand, Sir. Do you not remember how far the American business system crashed when the Arabs flew the planes into the twin towers in New York?"

"I do."

"Then what would happen to the American economy if a pandemic like the one we have suffered but on a larger scale were to infect America?" Husan asked.

"America is a long way off, Colonel. What kind of delivery system would we use? A missile?"

"Not a missile, Sir. A thousand missiles. Two legged missiles."

"Colonel, I do not care for cryptic conversations. Speak your mind or quit talking."

"Sir, do you have any idea how many people travel between China and the United States every month? Probably thousands, by air and by boat. What if each of those tourists and businessmen were given a souvenir to remember their trip to China? And what if all of those souvenirs were infected with our virus?"

Ming said, "We are not at war with the United States, Colonel!"

Husan stood behind his desk and raised his voice so quickly it startled Ming's companions. "A trade war is still a war, Mr. Ming. And we are involved in a trade war with the United States. And we are losing this war. Wars, Sir, are made to be won." He sat back down. "Tomorrow I shall complete my memo to my commanding general with part one, which I have just described to you. Part two would be to empty our jails and mental hospitals and give the people new identities and send them to U. S. ports on container ships to be smuggled into America. The people could ride on the ships in relative comfort and safety then, just before docking, they can be herded into containers as we have so often done in the past.

"While the ship is not infected, the containers they hide in will be. We can deliver, say, five containers to each major port, New York, Los Angeles, Seattle, San Francisco, Houston, New Orleans, the list goes on and on. In another month, we can send another load to help the pandemic along."

Ming asked, "Do you think your general and the politburo will agree to this?"

"I feel certain the general will. However, if I know him as well as I think I do, he will implement the program without telling anything to the politicians. If he decides to do it, that is," Husan said.

"Why are you telling me this, Colonel?"

"I believe, if my plan is accepted, your department will probably be tasked with carrying it out. By telling you about it now, you can start preparing your reply to the generals and not be surprised at the last moment. I plan to tell my general I have shared the plan with you. I do not know if he will tell that to the other generals. Expect my memo to my general to be delivered tomorrow by lunch time. I will not give you a copy unless my general instructs me to do so. I shall inform him I have shared this plan with you, but I will not put it in writing."

"Why not in writing?" Ming asked.

"If this is implemented without the knowledge of the politicians and later, they find out, plenty of heads will roll. Mine will roll for dreaming up the plan. Yours should not roll just because you heard about the plan and did not report it. It will be best for you to be able to claim you were not a part of the plan. If the plan works and they find out, you will be positioned to cash in on the political stroke it will give you by being the hero of the day."

The next day at 9:00 am, the three men walked into the lobby of the state-run mental health hospital near the center of Wuhan. The older of the three men showed the woman behind the desk a business card identifying him as the chief of the Beijing Bureau of Psychology Today Magazine and told her he wanted to see the hospital administrator to do a story about the "strides made by this hospital in the treatment of mental illness in China."

CHAPTER 10

Wuhan, Hubei District, China
January 10, 2020
2:00 pm, China Standard Time

The next day, Colonel Husan was making his afternoon rounds when he was interrupted by his secretary. "Excuse me, Colonel, Lieutenant General Chang is on the telephone holding for you. Do you want me to reroute the call to a phone in here?"

"No," Husan said. "I will take the call in my office. Put it through to my desk. Ask Lieutenant Ming to join me there."

When he reached his office, he closed his door but left it unlocked for Ming. He answered his phone and turned on the speaker feature. "This is Colonel Husan. How may I help you, Sir?"

"Husan, this is Chang. Are you alone?"

"I am, Sir. I have asked Lieutenant Ming to join me and he will be here shortly."

Chang asked, "Am I on a speaker phone?"

"Yes, Sir, General. Do you wish me to turn off the speaker?" Husan asked.

"No, no, let's leave it on. I want Ming to hear our conversation. Is he close by?"

Husan said, "I believe he is, Sir." At that moment, Ming walked into the office and closed the door behind him. He snapped to attention and said, "Lieutenant Ming reporting as ordered, Sirs."

Husan was silently making a signal to Ming as if he were holding a key, indicating he wanted Ming to lock the door. As Ming was doing that, Chang said, "You should lock your door, Husan."

Ming said, "I have just done that, Sir."

"Alright, gentlemen, you should probably sit and get comfortable. This is going to take a while." Both men sat,

Chang said, "Let us get straight to the reason I called. Colonel Husan, today I received your memo concerning your plan for unleashing the virus into the United States. I must say I am impressed with your work. Usually, these kinds of plans are the thought product of the security branch of the PLA. To have a medical administrator think them up is impressive. Did you have help with this plan, Husan?"

"No, General Chang. After I studied the results of the virus here locally, I saw the opportunity to fight back against the United States for the trade war their president is waging against us. It is my firm belief, Sir, we are losing this war. Chinese businesses are suffering under these restrictions and trade sanctions being enforced against us. As a military man first, and a doctor second, I believe a war is a war, whether we are attacked with missiles or with money, and wars are to be won, whatever the cost."

Chang said, "I can tell you are passionate about your plan, Colonel. However, I am not very enthusiastic about your plan to give infected souvenirs to visitors. That said, I want you to know I am very enthusiastic about your plan to send infected people to the United States on container ships. How would you keep them from infecting the crew and the rest of the ship?"

Husan said, "We would not infect the people we send; we

would put the virus in the containers. When the ship approaches the port, the people to be smuggled in would then get into the container. We would not tell them the container was infected. When they got to their destination, they would leave the container and spread out to their various destinations, leaving the container to do double duty as a source of infection for anyone encountering it." Husan paused for comments from Chang. There was none.

"We can send several containers to each major port, ensuring the virus will spread to a large cross section of citizens. Later, we can send another ship of containers to the same or to different ports."

Chang said, "Where do you suppose you will get the volunteers to let themselves be infected?"

"I have no intention of asking for volunteers or of telling them they will be infected. I believe we have enough undesirable people living in China that we can afford to lose a few."

Chang asked, "Who are these undesirable people and how will you convince them to go to America?"

"First," Husan said, "we can empty our mental hospitals of incurable people who are a drain on our resources. These people can be told they are going to America where they can receive better treatment than they can get here. They will probably have to be accompanied by trained mental health workers who will stay on the ship and come back to us."

"What else," Chang asked.

"After we rid our country of these useless citizens who are a drain on our resources, we then empty our prisons of the violent offenders who we do not want to release into our streets to prey on our innocent citizens," Husan said. "If they are reluctant to go, we can devise a fake escape plan in which they think they are being sent to some other location."

Chang asked, "Colonel, how long does it take for this virus to start spreading?"

Husan said, "About ten days, we think, Sir."

"During the ten days will not the crew of the ship get sick.?"

Husan replied, "No, Sir. My plan calls for none of the people to be infected either before boarding the ship or while on the ship during the voyage. Only the containers which will be used to smuggle them into the country will be infected. If they are detected, they will show no signs of the infection for ten days or so. I have tasked Lieutenant Ming with designing the inside of the containers so the infection will not escape. I have seen his preliminary drawings and I think he has excellent ideas."

Chang asked, "How will you be able to oversee this project and still complete your job in the lab?"

"I cannot do that, Sir. I have thought of the plan, but we need someone with experience in such plans to implement it, especially to point out any deficiencies," Husan said.

"And who do you recommend for the job, Colonel? Ming?"

"Yes, Sir."

"Really?" Chang asked. "Why Ming?"

"Not my Lieutenant Ming, Sir. I mean a Mr. Ming from the MSS. His section has great experience in what the Americans call 'dirty tricks'. I spoke briefly with him yesterday and we agreed the plan should be fine-tuned and implemented by his department. I also told him I was going to tell you I spoke to him, but I was not going to put anything in writing about him."

"Why?" Chang asked.

"Because, General, I realize the politburo does not see things the way the military does. They would prefer to end this trade war through endless negotiations with the Americans. Again, I believe we are engaging in a war and the politicians are going to be furious we did not notify them of our plans. I think there is no reason to risk Mr. Ming's career unnecessarily."

Chang was silent for a moment then said, "Why do you think I would proceed with a plan like this without clearing it with the Central Committee?"

Husan said, "General, I have served in the army with you for over twenty-five years. I think I know you well enough to know you find this to be an excellent plan, one which will be beneficial to our country."

Again, Chang was silent. "Colonel, by zero nine hundred tomorrow I want you and Lieutenant Ming to be in my office ready to present your plan, in detail, to the general staff. Lieutenant Ming, I want you to have at least some preliminary sketches ready when you get here."

Ming said, "I have already made detailed sketches and have prepared a cost estimate to convert up to ten containers and how many soldiers or others it will take to regulate the undesirables on the ship. I am also devising a cover story to be told to the undesirables and the crew of the ship."

"Great!" Chang said. "If you two can be here by zero seven hundred, I will feed you breakfast. Should I send a plane for you?"

"Oh, yes, Sir!" Husan said. "That would be wonderful."

"I will tell my pilot to be at your nearest airfield no later than zero-four-thirty. That should give you plenty of time. Do you think I should have Mr. Ming present?"

Husan answered, "I do not, Sir. I think it would be in

everyone's best interest if Mr. Ming did not appear at the same time as myself and Lieutenant Ming."

"Alright then," Chang said. "I will see you two in the morning. Will you need any AV equipment?"

"Just a projector," Husan said, "I will bring our own laptop."

The phone went dead. Ming said, "He surely doesn't waste any words on goodbyes, does he?"

"No, he doesn't," Husan said.

CHAPTER II

People's Liberation Army Headquarters
Beijing, China
January 11, 2020
7:50 am, China Standard Time

At 0075 the next day, Husan and Ming were escorted into the general's private dining room. Husan carried a laptop in a case and Ming brought a series of mounted sketches which he had concealed with a black cloth. As the three soldiers sat to eat, Chang asked, "Is there anything about this morning's meeting which we still need to discuss?"

Husan said, "I cannot think of anything, General. Ming and I talked during our plane ride and we could not think of anything more. By the way, I did insist your pilot show me his clearance card before we talked. I assumed since he was your pilot, he had such clearance, but I …"

Chang interrupted, "Flight officer Xin has been with me for over five years, and I trust him completely. He is privy to everything I say or do. Still, since you do not know him, you were wise to see his card. It shows me you are a thorough man.

"In the meeting this morning will be myself and five other generals. I thought it best to not include the generals from the Foreign Relations and the Management Divisions since they will probably not be involved in this operation. If necessary, I can always include them later if we need their services."

Ming asked, "How much time will we be allowed for our

presentation, Sir?"

"You may have whatever time you think necessary. While I have prepared an agenda, it is just a cover, and we will discuss nothing but Colonel Husan's plan. This is a specially called meeting and will not be reported to the Military Oversight Commission. Please understand, after this meeting, neither of you may speak about this plan to anyone unless I personally approve it."

"Yes, Sir," Husan said.

"Yes, Sir," Ming said.

"Also, there will be no secretary in the room and no notes will be made. From here forward, we will do everything verbally. There is to be no written communication," Chang said.

Husan said, "General, you speak as if the plan has already been approved."

"The plan was approved by me an hour after we spoke yesterday. Now, it is your job, both of you, to sell it to the rest of the generals. You did such a good job convincing me, these old war horses should be easily swayed. I am sure they will want you, Colonel, to be available to help Ming, the MSS Agent Ming, with any questions or problems implementing this plan. Also, they may want to know how long you think it will take to implement this plan. I would like to know that, too."

"I cannot give you a precise estimate on how long it will take," Husan said. "Most of that will depend upon Mr. Ming's department and their ability to implement the plan. They must find an appropriate ship, investigate it's crew, select the 'volunteers', etc. There will be a lot to do. I think a reliable and conservative estimate would be six to eight weeks for the first group to reach a U.S. port. However, I would prefer Mr. Ming make the estimate after he has reviewed the plan."

At exactly 0900 Chang, Husan and Ming walked into the conference room and found the other five generals waiting. Coffee was still being served. When the server finished pouring, he left the pot on the conference table and went out, locking the door behind him so the generals would not be interrupted. Chang gave a short opening statement, reminded the other generals of the security considerations of what they would discuss then turned the meeting over to Husan. Husan explained the basic points of his plan and opened the floor for questions. One of the generals asked, "What is to keep the infected 'volunteers' from dying before they get to the United States?"

Husan repeated the explanation he had given Chang. The "volunteers" would not be exposed to the corona virus until the day they were to disembark or the day before, whichever worked best.

That general asked how it would be done. Husan said, "Lieutenant Ming will show you his drawings and explain the mechanics of the containers."

Ming stood and placed his first drawing on an easel and said, "This is how the standard shipping container appears. As you can see in the picture, it is made of corrugated steel." He placed the second picture. "In this picture it shows how we would build an interior wall of plywood two inches inside the metal. Between the plywood and the metal will be a system of hoses with valves. This cutaway on the side shows how the hoses are placed."

He placed a third drawing on the easel. "This is a view of the backend of the container with a cutaway which shows an electric pump and a power source. Once all the volunteers are placed inside the container and it is sealed, one of the crew, a trusted member of Mr. Ming's staff, will insert a key into the small opening at the base of the container which will activate the pump and cause the odorless, colorless gas to seep gently into the container. The containers will be off-loaded onto trucks owned by one of our friends in the U. S. and dispersed throughout the region. By the time they are unloaded and opened, the volunteers will be fully infected and will spread out across the country, encountering as many people as they can."

Another general who looked like he did not like the plan said, "Colonel Husan, you say your 'volunteers' are to be recruited from mental hospitals and prisons. Have you no qualms about duping these poor people into being walking time bombs to die in a foreign country?"

The room was deadly silent as Husan rose to speak. Instead of addressing the one general, he addressed them all. "Gentlemen, we are at war. I know it is a trade war, but it is still a war. Instead of assaulting our citizens with missiles and bullets, the Americans are assaulting us with trade sanctions and economic policies. Our citizens, especially the small businesspeople and family-owned businesses, are starving to death under these sanctions. Make no mistake, a war is a war, and the Americans have started this war to try and force us into unfair trade agreements. You all know in wars, people die. The people I propose to send are not working, not building, not laboring; they are a drain on the resources of our country. Now, with the sanctions, our resources have become more precious. These people do not contribute to the welfare of the state. They simply drain what we have and give nothing back. The 'volunteers' from the mental hospitals will be people who have no idea of where they are or what they are doing. They can be told their families have emigrated to America and they are being smuggled in to join them. When they exit the containers in America, there will be no one there to greet them and they will begin to simply wander away.

"Do I have qualms about duping these people into our plan? Not at all. It is a choice we, rather you, must make. Do we place our interest in the volunteers or in our citizens who are contributing to our society?" He sat down.

The same general asked, "What about the criminals? How will you get them to comply?"

Husan stood again. "My suggestion is to take them ten or twelve at a time and convince them they are being smuggled out of the country in a clever escape. The problem with that is they must be guarded during the voyage. Their container will be the same as the other volunteers. I will leave the details of that part to Mr. Ming and his associates. They are better suited for that type of work than I."

"Tell me, Colonel, what kind of numbers do you expect to see and how much effect will it have on the economy there."

Husan rose again. "What we have seen in America so far, with the accidental spread of this virus, which is now called 'Covid-19', is over ten million people out of work. They are restricted to their home unless they have or work for an 'essential' business. An example of an essential business would be a hospital. Now, restaurants, bars, cinemas are all closed to stop the spread of the virus. The virus, or rather the economic fallout from the virus, has cost America hundreds of millions of dollars and thousands of deaths. If we can smuggle in ten of the converted containers, each with ten to twelve 'volunteers', by the end of the year America could be facing a loss of five hundred thousand to one million people. Such a loss would take years of recovery and economic hardship.

"When we see the plan succeeds, we can repeat it as many times as you generals care to do it, and we can sit back and watch America crumble."

A general asked, "Will not the collapse of the American economy also cause our economy to suffer?"

"I think it probably will," Husan said, "but not enough to throw out the whole plan."

There was a moment of silence. Another general said, "Colonel Husan and Lieutenant Ming, it is clear you have both made an excellent presentation after careful preparation. I applaud your professionalism."

General Chang stood and said, "The meeting is over. Colonel Husan and Lieutenant Ming, my pilot is waiting in my office to fly you back to Wuhan. Thank you for your presentation."

Husan and Ming snapped to attention and saluted General Chang. When he returned their salutes, they left the room, leaving the drawings behind. As they walked toward the office, Husan asked Ming, "Did you get the impression the general on the right end thinks I am a cold blooded, heartless monster?"

"I did, Colonel, but keep in mind, he is a general sitting here in this ivory tower building and does not see the things we see in the countryside and back roads of the country. He does not allow reality to corrupt his views and opinions." They both laughed.

On the plane ride back to Wuhan, Flying Officer Xin said, "You people in Wuhan cannot stand to not have non-controversial news, can you?"

"What do you mean?" asked Husan.

"Have you not heard the news today? Dr. Ling is missing!"

Xin said.

"Dr. Ling? Wasn't he the doctor who told the press about the spread of the corona virus?" asked Ming.

"He was," Xin answered. "I suspected he would be punished for his outburst. Maybe the MSS took him. Oh, well. He will probably turn up in a few days."

Husan and Ming stared silently at each other for a moment. Ming started to speak but Husan shook his head very gently. Both sat silent for the rest of the trip. When the plane landed in Wuhan, both men thanked Xin for a comfortable flight and left the plane. When they were in Husan's car, Ming said, "You do not really think Dr. Ling was arrested, do you?"

Colonel Husan said, "I think the next time anyone sees Dr. Ling he will not be breathing."

"I hope it does not happen to us if our part in the plan is revealed to the politburo," Ming said.

When they arrived at the lab it was almost 2100. They had waited until almost 1900 for the generals to come out of their meeting. As they walked down the circular stairs, Husan asked, "Why is there a light on in my office?" Ming drew his pistol and approached the door. He listened for any sounds then turned to Husan and said, "I hear a woman crying."

Husan motioned silently for him to open the door. When he did, the men saw Husan's secretary and niece, Wong Ja Man, sitting in Husan's chair behind his desk. She was startled for a moment then said, "Oh, Uncle, it is bad, bad, bad!" Husan moved past Ming and put his arm around Miss Wong's shoulder.

"There, there, Niece. What has happened that has upset you so?"

She said, "Do you remember my paternal grandmother?"

"I do," said Husan. "A wonderful old woman."

The girl stopped sobbing long enough to say, "She called me here yesterday and asked me to come by to see her after I finished my work here. I went to see her at her house which is directly across the road from the crematorium. She said she was sitting on her porch in the morning and several army trucks arrived across the street. She said the soldiers began unloading the white body bags from the trucks and taking them to the furnaces inside. Sometimes the workers there leave the outside doors open to help cool the place. She said there were fifteen trucks with ten to twenty bodies in each truck.

"She called me again this afternoon and told me she invited her neighbor to come sit with her so there would be another witness. I left work during my lunch period and drove to her house. She said, as she and her friend watched, the bodies in several of the bags started kicking and screaming. Then they threw those bags directly into the furnaces. I told her I would talk to you as soon as you returned because you would know what to do.

"When you did not return, I went back to her house and found two chairs overturned on the front porch. There was blood on the floor. Inside it looked like someone went crazy with an automatic weapon. There were bullet holes throughout the front room. There was blood on the floor, the walls and the furniture. I am so afraid for my grandmother. She is eighty-five years old and in poor health."

Husan patted the girl on the shoulder and said, "Tomorrow we will begin an inquiry about this. Until then, you will go to my house. I will tell your aunt you are spending a few days with us. Lieutenant Ming, would you please drive my niece to my house?

I will call my wife and tell her you are coming." He handed Ming his keys.

"Can't we just take my car?" Ja asked.

"No," Husan said, "If the soldiers are looking for whoever drove that car to your grandmother's house, it wouldn't do for them to find it at my house. Stay home tomorrow and Ming and I will start our inquiry in the morning."

Ming realized he was still holding his pistol. He holstered it and took Ja by the arm and led her up the stairs and into Husan's car. When Ming returned from delivering Ja to Colonel Husan's house, the colonel met him in the parking lot and got in on the passenger side. "Let us drive out to the crematorium and look at her grandmother's house."

When they arrived, they found the house with the lights on and the door open. Inside, they found the bullet holes and the blood just as Ja described. Husan walked into the only bedroom and found nothing disturbed. When he returned to the front room, he saw Ming staring out the front window. Ming said, "Sir, there is someone across at the crematorium and all the lights are on. He is loading bodies into the furnaces."

They drove across the road and approached the building. A very large man sweating profusely, approached the two as they walked to the door. In a very loud voice, the man yelled, "Get off my property, you worthless son-of-a-bitch, before I kick your ass and throw you in the furnace with all these others."

Ming began stripping off his coat and yelled back, "You and what army, you worthless piece of dog crap?" When the men were ten feet apart, they ran full speed at each other. Upon impact, instead of striking each other, they began hugging. Husan stood by confused. Ming said, "Colonel, this is my cousin

Quin on my mother's side." Quin nodded to Husan then said, "I am so glad to see you. I have been so sad this week I considered killing myself."

"Why would you consider such a thing, Quin?"

"Because three days ago a group of men told me you had died and I knew that meant I was now the ugliest man in China." They both laughed and hit each other on the bicep. Quin stopped and shook hands with Husan. He said, "Believe it or not, Colonel, when we were kids, we took turns beating the other up until our grandmother made us stop." Both men laughed.

Quin said to Ming, so what brings two army officers out late into the night. Checking up on your men?"

"My men?" asked Husan.

"Yes," Quin said. "Those men kept me busy all day and into the night. Bodies everywhere."

"Did the soldiers say where the bodies came from?" Huan asked.

"They did. They said there was a new outbreak of the…the…some kind of virus."

"The corona virus?" Ming asked.

"Yeah, but they said it's now known as Covid 19."

Husan asked, "Covid 19 virus?"

"No, the sergeant said it was now called 'Covid 19'. He didn't say the word virus with it."

"Where did all the bodies come from?" Ming asked.

"The sergeant told me they were people from nursing home who had already been infected, but…" He glanced at Husan.

Ming said, "You may speak in front of him. I guarantee your safety."

Quin said, "After all the soldiers left, there were seventy or so bodies left to be burned. The sergeant told me to burn them and to stay until they were all burned. I told him I was not authorized to stay because I would not get paid. The sergeant told me if I didn't do it, I might disappear and turn up in a few days floating face down in the Yangtze. So, here I am late at night burning bodies which were allegedly nursing homes patients who died from the virus. After the soldiers left, I noticed several of the body bags had blood on them. I opened a few here and there and found old people with bullet holes in their heads. Looking out the window, I noticed one of the body bags wiggling and screaming, a woman by the voice, and two soldiers threw it into the fire, and she screamed a lot more for a few moments then she was quiet and still." Quin sat down heavily on a nearby stool.

Husan asked, "Quin, did any of the soldiers go across the road to that yellow house?"

Quin said, "I didn't see them go across, but I heard a machine gun shooting and ran outside from my office. I saw one of the soldiers run back across the street and grab two body bags from one of the trucks. He ran back to the house and in a few moments, four soldiers carried two body bags in and laid them in front of the furnace. Both bags were bloody. They told me to load those two next." Quin began to sob heavily.

CHAPTER 12

FBI Headquarters
Chicago, Illinois, USA
January 11, 2020
10:22 am, Central Standard Time

Chris Weber sat in Ed Martin's office enjoying a cup of coffee. When Ed's cell phone rang, he glanced at the caller ID then immediately answered. "This is 546." He listened for a moment then said, "Hello, Bobby. How's tricks?" Again, he listened. "Hang on, Bobby, Chris is here in my office, and I want to put you on speaker so he can hear. Is that okay?"

Ed put the phone on the corner of the desk and pushed the button for the speaker. Chris said, "Good to hear from you, Bobby. Where are you?"

Bobby said, "Where I am is not important. Where I've been today, is."

Ed said, "Okay, Bobby, where have you been?"

"I just left Beijing about two hours ago, and I have big news. Important stuff. At nine this morning, China time, there was a meeting of six of the top nine generals of the PLA. They were presented with a plan from Colonel Husan and Lieutenant Ming of the lab under the chemistry building at Wuhan University."

"What kind of plan?" Chris asked.

"A plan to infect and kill hundreds of thousands of Americans with the Covid-19 virus."

"How do they plan to do that?" Ed asked.

"I don't have that yet. My guy in the general's office is trying to figure that out now. He knows it involves a container ship, but he doesn't know anything else."

Chris asked, "How did he get this info?"

"He is General Chang's pilot and the general sent him to fly Husan and Ming to Beijing for this meeting. They discussed the plan on the plane ride."

"Did they not try to keep him from hearing them?" Ed asked.

"No, they made him show his security clearance card and decided he was trustworthy."

"Bobby," Chris said, "can you trust this guy?"

"Well, he's worked for us for six years, he is a reliable conduit direct from the General to us, and one more thing, what was it? Oh, yeah, I'm married to his sister and I support his parents and family, anonymously, of course," Bobby said.

Ed asked, "When is this supposed to happen?"

"I'm still working on the when and the how. He did not get all the information. I should know more in a few days. He will contact his cousin who works on the docks in Shanghai. He also works for us. Sometimes I feel like I'm supporting the whole damn country."

Chris asked, "What can we do on our end, Bobby?"

Bobby said, "Ed, do you remember the guy who waited on us at the little restaurant on Archer Avenue in Chinatown?"

"You mean Oliver? The friendly waiter at Dolo's?"

"Yes. Go see him and give him my name and remind him you were there with me. Ask him to keep his ear to the ground for any info about an arrival of many Chinese being smuggled into the U. S. anytime soon."

"And if he does?" asked Chris.

"Ask him to give you a call and you will get the message to me. Tell him I'm out of town for a while."

"Got it," Ed said. "We'll try to get by there for an early lunch tomorrow."

Bobby said, "There's something you guys gotta really be aware of before you go there. This is life-saving information. Listen closely." There was a pause. "Are you listening?"

"Yes, Bobby," Chris said. "We're listening. What is it?"

"Whatever you do, do not order the Moo Goo Gai Pan. It really sucks. Go for the sweet and sour chicken or pork." They heard Bobby cackling like an old witch just before he disconnected.

CHAPTER 13

Wuhan, Hubei District, China
January 13, 2020
10:22 am, China Standard Time

Lieutenant Ming knocked on Colonel Husan's door and entered without waiting. Colonel, have you seen yesterday's copy of the afternoon newspaper?"

"I have not, Ming. What is in it?"

Ming said, "There is a front-page story there about how well Wuhan is recovering from the coronavirus pandemic. This is good news for our plan, is it not?"

"How so?"

"When the Americans see on television how Wuhan, 'ground zero' of the pandemic is recovering so quickly, they will start to relax and be more careless about social distancing and other habits. They will ease the spread of the second round which we send over. That will give our 'volunteers' a better chance of infecting more people."

Husan took the paper from Ming and quickly scanned the article. While still reading, he felt for his phone and dialed his secretary. "Please get Lieutenant General Chang on the phone. Tell them it is urgent and cannot wait. If he is not in, find out where he is and track him down. Burn up the telephone line until you have him on the phone. Tell General Chang something has arisen that may alter 'The Plan'." He hung up the phone and looked at Ming.

"If we can move quickly enough, we may be able to capitalize on this temporary lapse in America's defensive posture. We need to discuss whether we want to send more than ten containers now." His intercom beeped and his secretary said, "Sir, General Chang is on line two."

Smiling as he picked up the phone, Husan said, "Good morning, General Chang. Yes, Sir, it is urgent." He listened for a moment. "Sir, Lieutenant Ming has brought to my attention a story in yesterday afternoon's paper here in Wuhan about the great strides our city has made in returning to normalcy after the pandemic. Were you aware of this?" Pause. "Yes, Sir, that is the story I mean." Pause. "General, Lieutenant Ming had the idea if the Americans are seeing this story on their news, it might have the effect of them letting their guard down." Silence. "My question is, General, if we find this to be true, first, should we try to increase the 'volunteers' in the first wave and, second, what would be the logistical problem of converting another eight or ten or more containers?" He listened again. "Sir, may I be so bold as to suggest that you contact Mr. Ming and get his opinion on this?" He listened again. "Yes, Sir. I will tell him. Thank you, General."

As the Colonel was hanging up the phone, on the other side of the world in Chicago, Ed and Chris were walking into Dolo's restaurant. Ed told the Maître-d they wanted to sit in Oliver's section. He said something in Chinese to the hostess who led them to a table. When she walked away, Ed asked, "What did he say to her?"

"Take these guys to number 11,"

"Oh," Ed said.

When Oliver arrived Ed said, "Bobby told me to avoid the Moo Goo Gai Pan. Is that true, Oliver?" Oliver studied Ed for a moment then said, "Oh, I remember you. You were here with Bobby not too long ago."

"Right. Oliver this is my partner, Chris. We BOTH work with Bobby."

"What may I serve you gentlemen?"

Ed said, "I'm gonna have the sweet and sour chicken with fried rice and an egg roll.

Chris said, again in perfect Mandarin, "Oliver, I will have the sweet and sour pork, also with fried rice and two egg rolls. And some hot tea, please."

Oliver turned and walked away without asking if there was anything else. A few minutes later, Oliver returned with soup and egg rolls. As he placed the food on the table, he asked, "Is Bobby coming to join you?"

"No," Chris said. "Bobby is out of town for a few days but asked us to stop in and ask you a question."

Oliver asked, "What is it?"

"Bobby wants to know if you've heard anything about an unusually large number of Chinese nationals being smuggled in on a container ship. And if you hear anything would you please call Ed here and let him know so he can pass the info on to Bobby?"

"I have heard nothing yet," Oliver said. "I will ask around to see if any of my brothers know of anything. By the way, your mandarin is superb. Not many round-eyes can do that."

"I had a good teacher, Oliver. After my mother died, my dad remarried when I was six years old. My stepmother was from the Hubei District of China. Oliver disappeared and returned a few minutes later with the rest of their food. He picked up Ed's business card from the table and slipped it into his vest pocket.

CHAPTER 14

City Docks
Shanghai, China
January 23, 2020
9:11 AM, China Standard Time

Flight Officer Xin stood in front of General Chang's desk at attention. As the general sat, he said, "Relax. Stand easy. I have an important mission for you. I want you to fly to Shanghai and seek out Mr. Ming of the MSS. Do you remember him, know what he looks like?"

"Yes, Sir."

"I want you to memorize the questions on this paper then destroy it. Then go to Shanghai and ask Ming these questions. Wait for his answers then fly directly back here. Do you understand?"

"Yes, Sir."

"Go, go. I want his answers by tonight."

As he drove to the airstrip, Xin thought, 'I guess figuring out the when and how just got easier'. When he arrived in Shanghai, a car met him at the airport. At the docks, the driver led him to the shop area and Xin saw a line of ten containers with the doors open. The driver pointed out Mr. Ming who was involved in a conversation with a worker. When he finished the conversation, Ming approached Xin who came to attention and saluted. Ming said, "We do not salute here. We do not reveal our rank. It makes it easier when we must investigate someone of a higher rank.

Now, what can I do for you?"

Xin explained the reason for his trip and asked all the questions the general wanted answered. He even threw in a few questions he or Bobby wanted to know.

Ming took him into one of the containers which had been fitted with hoses, pump, power source and connection for the bottle of the corona virus, all of which had not yet been covered by the plywood. Xin made a mental note of everything he was told and shown. When he was again airborne, he put the plane on autopilot and began writing everything Mr. Ming had told or shown him and drew a sketch of the dispersal system. When he landed in Beijing he went immediately to General Chang's office and reported everything Ming had said.

The general said, "Good work, Xin. I can always depend upon you. As he finished his oral report, the phone rang and Chang answered, "General Li, I was just about to call you." Xin rose to leave, but Chang motioned for him to stay.

Chang listened for a moment them said, "The name of the ship is the Shanghai Lady and it will leave shortly after midnight." He listened for another moment then said, "Where? I do not know. Let me ask Xin." Without covering the phone, Chang asked Xin, "Do you know the first port they will stop at and how long it will take to get there?"

Xin said, "It will take from two weeks to a month to get there, depending on the typhoon. However, I have no idea of the first stop. Ming would not tell anyone, even his own men."

An hour later, Xin was on the phone with Bobby and giving him the information, he had. Bobby said, "We can track the ship with the satellite until it gets deep into the typhoon, but we may lose it there. Since we do not know the first stop, we will be forced to intercept it in international waters. That will be dicey. Now we know the name of the ship, we can identify her on sight. Sure wish we knew where that thing was headed."

Xin said, "I will keep listening to see if anyone mentions where the first port is, I may be in a position to hear. However, I do not feel positive about that."

"Okay," Bobby said. "Great work, Xin. Let me know as soon as you hear something else." Bobby disconnected.

CHAPTER 15

Beijing, China
January 23, 2020
2:30 PM

Xin sat in his car talking on his cell phone. He told Bobby, "They are trying to move up the departure date to three days from today. General Chang said that since the news is talking about Wuhan's recovery going so well, the news reporting in America will be the same. It may make Americans feel more relaxed, and they may let their guard down. Someone, probably Husan, wants to add more containers to the first shipment, but Mr. Ming said the general can have his choice. He can have more containers, or he can move up the date of departure. He cannot have both.

Bobby asked, "Do you know the name of the ship yet?"

"No," Xin said. "Ming got very uneasy when I asked and wanted to know why the general wanted to know. I told him knowing the general's mind is not one of my duties. He did not tell me the name of the ship."

"Do we know how long it takes a container ship to go from Shanghai to the west coast of the U. S.?" Bobby asked.

"I do not know, but I will find out," Xin said.

About that time, Ed Martin received a telephone call from Oscar who had some information for him, but he did not want to reveal it over the phone. He asked Ed to meet him behind the restaurant in one hour. Ed called Chris and said, "Oscar wants to talk to us in person. We're going to meet him behind the restaurant in one hour. I'll meet you at your car."

When they arrived at the back of the restaurant, they did not see Oscar at first. They walked to the far end of the restaurant where they found him sitting on the ground with his back against the building. His white shirt was drenched in blood and his throat was cut. The agents quickly went through his pockets but found nothing which would indicate what he wanted to tell them. Ed dialed 9-1-1, identified himself and reported a dead body. They stayed at the scene waiting for Chicago P. D. to arrive. While waiting, Chris said, "Ed, do you notice anything strange about Oscar?"

Ed studied the body for a few seconds then asked, "Strange like what?"

Chris said, "From the moment I met Oscar inside the restaurant, I was impressed by how fastidious he was. But now there seems to be something out of place or out of balance, and I can't put my finger on it. He just looks...out of balance. I don't know how else to describe it."

Ed walked to where Chris was standing, and they both stared at Oscar's body. After a moment. Ed said, "It's his button!"

"What button?" Chris asked.

"Second button, from the top."

"What about it?" Chris asked.

"It's different, a different style."

Chris walked closer to the body and stooped. "Because it's not a button, Partner, it's a lens!"

"A lens? Like a camera lens?"

"Yep," Chris said. "Our favorite Chinese waiter is wearing a buttonhole camera." Chris began rifling through Oscar's pants pockets but found nothing. He searched inside the waistband of Oscar's pants and found the small digital video recorder. He removed the recorder and pulled the wire leading from Oscar's waistband to the buttonhole camera, pulled a switchblade from his own pocket and carefully cut the camera lens from the shirt. Chris wound the lens and wire around the recorder and stuffed all of it in his coat pocket just as the first Chicago P.D. unit arrived on the scene.

Chris and Ed both showed their IDs and badges and told the patrol officers they were supposed to meet Oscar and found him dead. That he didn't say what he wanted to talk to them about. So there was nothing else to tell them. Ed said, "Here is my card and I wrote my cell number on the back. Tell your detectives to call us if they have any questions."

When they drove away from the restaurant, Ed called Bobby and told him what happened. Bobby said, "Oh, man. He was my best contact in Chinatown. It will take me years to groom another. While I have you on the phone, the container ship will sail in four days. I still do not know the name of the ship. General Chang wanted to add more containers and more people, but Mr. Ming said he couldn't add more people without delaying the departure date. The news accounts of Wuhan recovering from the epidemic virus has inspired Lieutenant Ming to think Americans will now let their guard down, thinking they are nearing the end of the pandemic. However, the news stories are false, planted by the MSS.

Bobby asked, "How long before you can see what's on that buttonhole camera?"

"I'll drop it at the tech department when we get back to the office in about twenty minutes. I have no idea how long it will take them to pull some video from it," Chris said. "I'll let you know as soon as I see it."

At the office, Chris told Ed, "I'm going to drop this camera off to the techs and try to get some idea about when they can have the images ready to view. I'll meet you in your office." At the lab, Chris looked for Judy, his favorite tech and asked, "How soon can you get me some video off this thing?"

Judy took the camera and examined it. "Chris, why is this unity wet?" Did you drop it in the water?"

"It's not water, Judy, it's blood."

"Well, crap", Judy said. She opened a drawer in the desk and removed a pair of latex gloves and a plastic evidence bag. She handed the bag to Chris and said, "Fill this out." Chris wrote on the label of the evidence bag then handed it back to Judy. After glancing at the information on the label, Judy asked, "What kind of case number is 'Mongoose'? It's not one of our case numbers."

"No, it's not," Chris answered.

"Chris, I can't log this in without a case number."

"No, Judy, you can't… and you won't."

"But, Chris…"

Chris interrupted. "Judy, I'm the ASAC in this office. If I tell you to forget the case number, you can forget the case number. Now when can I get it back?"

"I suppose you need this yesterday, right?"

"Judy, the lives of thousands of Americans are resting on what you might find on that contraption. I need it the day before yesterday."

Judy turned and walked away. Over her shoulder, she said, "I'll call you. And you are going to owe me a steak dinner for this."

"Great," Chris said. "You pick the restaurant, and my wife and I will meet you there."

"You know you're a horse's butt, don't you, Chris?"

"Yes, Ma'am," Chris said as he left the lab.

CHAPTER 16

Shanghai, China
January 24, 2020
3:43 am, China Standard Time

Bobby's cell phone rang at 0343. "Hello."

Xin said, "The name of the ship is the 'Shanghai Lady' and she sails in four days. There is a typhoon building in the Pacific and her captain plans to sail right through it."

"Great, Xin. Where are they headed?"

"Nobody knows," Xin answered. "Ming is the only one who knows, and he won't even tell the captain until after they sail."

Bobby said, "I thought ships had to notify the port authorities, kind of like an aircraft must file a flight plan before they take off."

Xin answered, "Keep in mind, Bobby, this is a government operation, a secret operation, and this is China," Xin said. "These guys can do just about anything they want."

"Thanks, Xin. Keep trying to learn the first port on the 'Shanghai Lady's' itinerary. If you get it, call me, day or night, I don't care." Bobby disconnected and immediately called Ed.

"Hello, partner. How goes things in...in...wherever the hell you are?" Ed said.

"Xin discovered the name of the ship. It's the 'Shanghai Lady' and it sails in four days. We still don't know where it's headed."

Ed said, "Bobby, Chris just walked in. I'm going to put you on speaker. Is that alright?"

Bobby said, "Sure. That's fine."

Chris asked, "What have you got for me, Bobby?" Bobby gave Chris the same information he gave Ed.

Chris said, "Well I've got some info for you. I just came from our tech section. The hidden camera Oscar had on him was working fine. It turns on when Oscar is walking to the back of the restaurant where he waits for us, he is approached by what we thought at first was two men. Turns out one was a woman. The woman says 'Hello, Oscar. We need to talk.'

Oscar says, "Who are you? I do not know you."

The woman said, "But I know you, Oscar. Our friends in Beijing think you are asking too many questions about people coming to America. You should stop asking these questions,"

Oscar said, "This is America, not China. Here I can ask or say anything I want. I will not stop, and you cannot make me stop. Now go away, I have business here."

"So do I," the woman said. Her right hand moved swiftly swinging the carpet knife so precisely Oscar's throat and juggler vein were opened, and Oscar fell against the wall bleeding to death in seconds.

Chris said, "The lab is using our facial recognition software trying to match the killers' faces, but it could take a while."

"Okay," Bobby said, "Keep me updated on it, please."

"Will do," Chris said. "In the meantime, what are we going to do about the lady from Shanghai?"

Bobby said, "If we can't track the ship via satellite, we'll have to intercept her in American waters. Can we do it?"

Ed said, "I don't know if we can find her coming out of the typhoon."

Chris said, "Ed, can the general get us a submarine?"

"You know how to drive a sub, Chris?"

"No," Chris answered. "I'm talking about a Navy sub, complete with a crew."

"Who is the general?" Bobby asked.

Chris said, "It's above your security clearance level, Bobby. Besides, no one here can answer that question."

Ed said, "Okay, Bobby. We'll keep you posted," Bobby disconnected.

Ed immediately punched a preset digit on his cell phone and waited for someone to answer. When they did, Ed said, "This is Ed Martin, 546. Connect me with the general." After a wait of about five seconds, the general answered. "This is the General, Ed. What can I do for you?"

Ed said very calmly, "General, we, Chris and I, need a submarine in the Pacific Ocean. We've got to get eyes on the ship before she gets to American waters."

The general said, "That's a tall order, Ed. It may take a while."

"Okay, Sir, but we've only got three days left."

"I'll call you back," the general said.

"How long will this take?" Chris asked.

"Getting an active Navy sub loaned to us by the United States Navy, would be a nightmare for a normal person. It will probably take the general up to fifteen minutes."

Before he could speak again, Ed's phone rang. Ed answered and listened for about fifteen seconds. He disconnected and asked, "Chris, do you still keep a packed bag in your truck?"

"I do," Chris answered. "Why?"

Ed walked to his closet, retrieved an overnight bag, and said, "Cause we're on our way to Pearl Harbor. Our flight leaves O'Hare in thirty minutes. They'll hold the flight for us."

As they walked toward the parking garage, whatshername

opened her door and leaned out into the hallway. "Chris, I've got something for you on the Mongoose lady. Both men turned and followed her into the lab, closing the door behind them.

Whatshername said, "It took a while, but I finally got a hit on the facial recognition software. She brought an image up on her computer screen. This is the woman who killed Oscar. Next to it, on a split screen, show showed an image of an Asian woman in an airport. "This woman identified herself as Emily Lyn. She entered the country at San Francisco two weeks ago. One her visa application, she denied ever being in the military of a foreign country. She projected a third image of the same woman, this time dressed in the uniform of an officer in the MSS. This is a picture from two years ago of Captain Emily Lyn, whose latest assignment was to locate Lieutenant Qui or his body. Apparently, she had one more task to complete and that was to kill Oscar while she was here.

"Bureau agents in San Francisco found her hiding in the Chinese consulate last night. This morning she was arrested for falsifying information on her visa application They are holding her for you."

Chris drove as fast as he could without causing a wreck or a speeding ticket while Ed stayed on the phone changing their flight to one headed to San Francisco which gave them an extra six minutes to get to the airport. They were met at the door by a woman in the airline's uniform who escorted them through the security checkpoint and to the door of the plane. A flight attendant said, "I'm sorry, gentlemen, your call came in so late the only seats available are in first class. I hope that will be alright," Chris said, "We'll find a way to get through it. It'll be tough, but we're tough, too." When they had settled in, the plane took off.

Chris asked, "Hey. I forgot to ask. Where are we going again?"

"Pearl Harbor via San Francisco."

"And when we get there?" Chris asked.

Ed said, "There will be a submarine waiting for us to go look for the 'Shanghai Lady' somewhere in the Pacific Ocean."

"I got a text message from the general about that." He showed Chris the screen on his phone. The message read, "If you find the lady, you are authorized to order the Captain to send her down."

"You going to do it?"

"Let's wait until we find her before we make that decision. How do you feel about the message, Chris?"

"Personally, I feel it's a good decision. We have an attack on our country by a rogue group, and we have got to stop it from happening. Whatever we must do, we must do."

When they landed in San Francisco, they were met at the airport by an FBI agent who drove them the local headquarters. When they arrived, the ASAC told them that the woman refused to answer any questions and insisted on seeing the Chinese consul before she would talk.

Ed gave her the same spiel Bobby had given Qui about the patriot act and told her she would have no contact with anyone until the FBI and the CIA and any other alphabet agencies were finished interrogating her at whatever location they felt like sending her to and that could take at least one hundred-eight days. He told her that she had violated at least eleven sections on the U. S. Code plus espionage then the local laws like murder and conspiracy to commit murder. He also said that if she refused to give any information she would be released with no charges and that action would be accompanied by a press release explaining that she had been "extremely cooperative" in providing information that could be used to stop Chinese espionage activities in the U. S. and in Wuhan, China.

When Ed mentioned Wuhan, the woman's eyes widened and filled with fear. She told Ed she wanted to speak to him privately and begged him not to let her go because it would mean a death sentence for her. Ed informed her he did not care and stood to leave. The woman started stammering and speaking in a mixture of Chinee and English but Ed and Chris rose and left her chained to the desk, screaming at the two men to stop and listen to her.

Outside the interview room, Ed told the local agent to wait twenty-four hours than turn her over to the local espionage task force and they could call Ed if they needed anything further. "When you're finished with her, Chicago P. D. will want to talk to her about Oscar's murder.

From the FBI office, the two were returned to the airport and flew to Honolulu where they were met at the airport shortly after 0130 by a petty officer who drove them to the Pearl Harbor Navy Base where they were stopped at the gate. When the gate guard came out of his small office with a clip board, the petty officer rolled down his window and handed the guard a clipboard. The guard returned to the office where he handed the clipboard to a Navy Commander wearing a camo uniform. The commander walked out of the building and got into the front seat next to the petty officer. He showed something on the clipboard to the petty officer who drove forward into the base.

Shortly after they started moving, Chris saw a navy jeep with two armed shore patrolmen pull out in front of them. Another similar jeep followed behind. After a fifteen-minute drive, the little convoy stopped at a wharf where a submarine was docked.

CHAPTER 17

United States Navy Base
Pearl Harbor, HI, USA
January 24, 2020
6:22 pm, Hawaii-Aleutian Standard Time

The two agents approached the officer at the foot of the gangway who said, "I will need IDs from both of you gentlemen." While they waited for the man to record the information from the two men, Chris noticed that the boat's name and ID number had been painted over.

The officer recorded their names and other information on a form on his clipboard then returned them to the agents. "Gentlemen, we are about to shove off. We were just waiting for you to arrive. If you will follow me, I will show you to your quarters" As they walked, the officer talked to them. "We have moved a junior officer to share a room with another officer and the two of you will share his room." The men followed the officer through a door in the side of the sail and down a ladder to the main control room. From there, he led them towards the front of the boat and down another ladder. There was a short walk down a narrow hallway, and they arrived at their room. The officer held back the curtain for them to enter.

Ed asked, "No doors on subs?"

"Not for junior officers," he said. "There is really no privacy on a submarine. You know everybody's business, and everybody knows yours. You gentlemen will wait in this room until the

Captain is ready to see you. Someone will fetch you for meals, and you are advised to talk to nobody but the captain about your mission and to report to the captain anyone who asks any questions about the mission.

"Now that I have talked your ears off, is there any question I can answer about living aboard a submarine?"

Ed said, "I've got a question. Where is the bathroom?"

"We do not have bathrooms. We have heads. The nearest one to your room is around the corner to the left and it is the third door on the right. The instructions are on the wall,"

"Okay." Ed said. "I'm going there right now. You gentlemen can carry on without me."

As he was leaving the room, Chris asked, "What is your name, Lieutenant?"

"I am sorry, I thought I had introduced myself. I suppose I was in a hurry to get you logged in and was feeling rushed. My name is Richard Landers, Lieutenant Richard Landers."

The men shook hands, and Landers left the room. Chris lay on the bunk and felt the movement of the sub as it made a sharp turn to the left. He thought to himself it was the wrong direction. He sat up as Ed walked in. "Chris, did you just feel something like the boat making a turn?

Chris said, "I did."

"And did it seem to you we turned in the wrong direction?"

"It did", Chris said. "Get your tablet out and bring up a map of the north Pacific."

When the map was up, they looked at the close-up version and saw the layout of the navy base. Chris said, "If we draw an imaginary line between us and Shanghai, turning left out of the gate like that would be a wrong turn. We need to ask the Captain when we see him. I imagine he will be busy until we are fully under way. And I imagine it will be long enough for a little nap. You want the folding bed or the bunk?"

Ed answered, "I don't care, Chris. You're already on the bunk so why don't you just keep it?"

Chris stretched on the bunk and said with a smile, "You talked me into it, you silver-tongued devil, you."

Chris had just lay down when there was a knock on the wall next to the doorway. "Come in," Ed said.

A young sailor in dungarees pushed the curtain aside and said, "Gentlemen, the Captain will see you now. I'm to escort you to his cabin." He led the two agents up a ladder, through the control room and down a hall toward the front of the boat. The sailor stopped at a door and knocked. They heard someone say, "Enter" and the sailor opened the door and escorted the men inside.

The Captain said, "Thank you, Ricks. That will be all."

The sailor said, "Aye, Captain," and left the room, closing the door behind him.

The Captain introduced himself as Durwood Tennyson and the other officer as his XO, Commander Fritz Tucker. The four men sat at a table and the Captain said, "Okay, I am going to tell you my orders, and I want you to fill in the gaps, okay?"

"Okay," Chris said. "Shoot."

Tennyson said, "I am ordered to pick you up during the hours of darkness at a dock nowhere near the submarine bays, which I have done, and to travel by a circuitous route to a point in the Pacific ocean which is nowhere near any land and to search for a container ship named the Shanghai Lady."

"Yes, Sir, Captain," Ed said. That is our understanding also."

"And if we find that ship?" asked the captain.

Chris said, "Captain, it is imperative we find that ship before it reaches American waters. Aboard that ship are certain containers which contain biologic materials being sent to attack U. S. citizens on U. S. soil. Unfortunately, we do not know the ship's first port of call."

The XO asked, "What kind of biologic materials are we talking about, Agent Weber?"

"At this point we are not at liberty to divulge that. What we want to do is to first, find her, then track her until we receive further orders. I anticipate those further orders will answer your questions."

Ed added, "Captain, for a while now Agent Weber and I have been assigned to a joint task force with the FBI, the CIA and the Army. The CIA has done extensive work, dangerous work, on the ground inside China. The work has resulted in the arrest or death of several members of the Chinese Army operating within the U. S."

Captain Tennyson said, "I do not mind telling you gentlemen I do not like being ordered to take this boat directly into the middle of a typhoon to search for a private commercial vessel."

Chris said, "Captain, I can understand your reluctance to do so, but if this mission fails, we are looking at the loss of half a million or more American lives."

The Captain's mouth fell open. "Are we talking about a nuclear bomb?"

"No, Sir," Ed said quickly. "I think we are safe to tell you this is a biological weapon."

"Crap," the XO said.

Tennyson asked, "Were either of you gentlemen in the

military?"

"Eight years in the Army, West Point class of 2012."

Ed added, "I was Marine recon in Desert Storm. Two tours."

"Well," the Captain said. "At least they didn't send us some damn civilians."

"Two more things we should discuss, Captain," Chris said.

"Go ahead."

"First, when we left Pearl, It felt like we turned left instead of right. Was that for the circuitous route your orders called for?"

"It was," the Captain said. "And the other?"

"I am assuming, on a U. S. nuclear submarine, you operate with a constant and heightened sense of security."

"Twenty-four/seven," The XO said.

Ed added, "It is my understanding this is an extremely sensitive and top-secret operation. Are you going to be able to keep your crew silent about what happens on this mission?"

The XO said, "Every member of this crew has a high level of security clearance. There will be no loose talk, I guarantee it."

"Then I guess we have nothing else we need to discuss until we find the Shanghai Lady."

The discussion was interrupted by a knock on the door. "Enter," the Captain said.

Lieutenant Landers came in holding a sealed yellow envelope on a clipboard which he handed to the Captain. After signing an acknowledgement and opening the message he read it, then handed it to the XO. To Landers, he said, "Plot an intercept course."

Landers said, "Aye, aye, Captain," and left the room. The XO handed the message to Ed who shared it with Chris.

"Your Shanghai Lady has been located by a satellite about

one-hundred miles southwest of our current position. Once the navigator plots the intercept course, we will have a better idea of how long it will take to reach her."

Ed asked, "Once we reach her and follow her will your folks be able to figure out where she's headed?"

"Sort of," Tennyson said.

"Sort of?" Chris asked.

"If she steams in a straight line for a long time, we can make an educated guess, but you never know where she might make a few turns here and there just to throw us off." The captain stood. "I will send for you when we are closer to the intercept."

Ed asked, "How can I make a phone call from the boat?"

The XO, who had just returned to the room, laughed. "We don't exactly have a long telephone wire following behind us. You will have to make your communication via email. Will that work for you?"

"Well," Ed said, "if that's all I've got, I guess it will have to do."

"When you're ready to send it, I'll have a technician come to your berth and show you how our system works."

"Thanks," Ed said, and he and Chris left the room. In the hallway outside, the same sailor who escorted them to the Captain's cabin was there to escort them back. "As they waited in their cabin, Ed composed an email to the general. He asked Chris, "Did you get the impression we might have some trouble convincing our Captain to fire torpedoes into an unarmed commercial vessel?"

"I certainly did, but how are we going to alert the general to that when the Captain will probably read every email we send or receive?"

Ed said, "I found it advantageous several years ago to create a code only the general, Bobby and I know. It isn't elaborate but will probably thwart the average code breaker for a day or two. I plan to use that."

Lieutenant Landers poked his head through the curtain. "Gentlemen, we will intercept the Shanghai Lady in eight hours and thirty-two minutes." He left without waiting for a reply.

CHAPTER 18

Pacific Ocean
Latitude 28.437833, Longitude 158.765822
January 24, 2020
11:43 pm, Kamchatka Time (PETT)

The same escort sailor knocked and entered the cabin. "Gentlemen, the Captain would like for you to join him in the control room. When they arrived, the Captain asked them to join him at a map table. He showed them their position and that of the Shanghai Lady. Chris asked, "Has she maintained a steady course?"

"Absolutely not," said the Captain. "She has turned to port, turned to starboard, even made a circle once. Looks like she is expecting to be followed."

"Well," Ed said. "I guess she is not going to give us a clue about where she is headed. How's the storm up top?"

"Still blowing. It seems like the farther we go, the more the storm closes around us," the XO said.

Ed and Chris shared a look, then Chris said, "Captain, can we speak privately?"

"Follow me to my cabin, Gentlemen. XO, join us please."

Inside the Captain's cabin, Chris said, "Captain, we need you to sink that ship."

The Captain took a half step backwards. "Sink an unarmed commercial vessel? Are you out of your mind?"

Chris said, "Captain, were you not ordered to take your

instructions from us?"

"That doesn't include murdering innocent civilians!"

Chris said, "Captain, there are no innocent civilians on that ship. That ship is being operated by a faction of the Chinese Liberation Army and is on the way to the U. S. to release dozens of Chinese nationals infected with the corona virus, Covid-19. Those people will infect hundreds of thousands of unsuspecting Americans and ruin our economy. I need you to put two torpedoes into her, one fore and one aft so she sinks in the shortest time possible. And while she is sinking, I need you to jam her communications so she cannot report she has been torpedoed.

"As soon as she is under, I need to broadcast an SOS pretending to be her radio operator."

"You are out of your freakin' mind," the XO said.

The Captain said, "You can forget your crazy plan. It is NOT going to happen."

Chris said, "Is that your final answer, Captain?"

"It is."

"Then can we continue to follow her for the time being?" Chris asked.

"We can."

As they left the Captain's cabin, Chris said, "Send your email, Ed."

When they returned to their cabin, it took Ed only seconds to send the email he had already composed. "I'm betting more than ten but less than twenty," Ed said.

Chris asked, "More than ten but less than twenty what?"

"More than ten minutes but less than twenty minutes until our Captain receives orders to sink the Shanghai Lady."

"Oh, no," Chris said. "I'm not taking that bet. I've seen how your general operates." Both looked at their watches. In thirteen minutes, the escort sailor knocked again. "Gentlemen…"

"We know, we know. The Captain would like for us to join him in his cabin. We know the way."

"I still have to escort you, Sir. Security regulations since you are not part of the crew."

In the captain's cabin, the XO closed the door and bolted it behind them. Without a word, the captain handed them a message and said, "Top secret, eyes only. If you will look at the header on this message, you will see it is direct to me from POTUS. I have never in my career received a message from the President of the United States, especially one that skips everyone between him and me in the chain of command. I would love to keep it as a souvenir, but the message orders me to destroy this message as soon as I have read it and to delete it from all archives on the boat. Let me read it to you. Attention to orders."

Both the Captain and the XO stood to attention. "It is addressed to me aboard this boat and says, quote, "You are ordered to intercept the container ship Shanghai Lady and without warning, repeat, WITHOUT WARNING, sink the Shanghai Lady by firing one torpedo into her fore hull and another torpedo into her aft hull, simultaneously if possible, so the vessel sinks in the shortest amount of time. Immediately preceding the firing of the torpedoes, you are to jam all radio communications from said vessel so no distress call can be sent. Once the vessel has sunk, you will make available to Assistant Special Agent in Charge, Chris Weber, any communications equipment aboard your submarine so he may send any messages he desires. You will coordinate all subsequent activities with

Weber until your return to Pearl Harbor. It is signed by the president."

Chris said, "Thank you, Captain. How long until we are in position to fire?"

Tennyson glanced at the XO who looked at his watch and said, "Twelve minutes."

The Captain said, "Would you go ahead to the control room and get everything set up?"

"Yes, Sir," the XO said and left the cabin without looking at either agent.

"Why are you going to send a radio message after the ship is under?" the Captain asked Chris.

"The Chinese officer named Ming who is heading up this mission knew there was a typhoon out here but chose to ignore it. I want to convince the folks back in China the ship was sunk by the storm, not a U. S. Navy sub. If I wait until just after she goes under, I can pretend to be their radio operator and call an SOS saying the ship is taking on water through a split in the hull. After I say my part, in perfect Mandarin, I will cut off the transmission abruptly and let the home folks think the ship broke up in the storm."

The Captain thought for a moment and said, "That might work, but I still do not like it."

"I understand, Captain. This is not our first choice either, but it is necessary. Also, I request the four of us reconvene here when it is over."

"For what reason?"

"When it is over, I will be able to share more information with you."

"Okay," the Captain said. "Let's go to the control room."

When he entered the control room, the XO handed the Captain the mike for the PA system. The Captain looked at the mike and shook his head. "The less said, the better. Weapons officer, I want to know as soon as we are at optimum shooting position."

"Aye, Captain," came the reply from someone Chris could not see. There was silence for a moment then the man said, "Optimum range now, Captain."

The Captain walked over to the weapons control panel and, instead of telling the sailor there to fire, the Captain pushed a button and the sailor said, very quietly, "One fired electrically." When the Captain pressed the second button, the sailor said, again quietly, "Two fired electrically."

The Captain returned to the center of the bridge where the XO was raising the periscope. He looked through it, then let the XO verify the sinking. "Agent Weber, if you will step over to the console behind you, Seaman Beaumont will provide you with a microphone to send your message. Chris keyed the mike and began yelling and jabbering in Mandarin. Every once in a while, he would switch to pidgin English but then switch back to Mandarin. After about five minutes, he abruptly stopped.

The Captain said, "XO will you please join us in my cabin?" The four men walked to the Captain's cabin and locked the door.

Chris said, "Ed, do you want to start?"

The two agents told the entire story, taking turns covering all the details. "You see, Captain, this doctor at the University in Wuhan came up with this plan to retaliate against the U. S. for the economic war we were waging against his beloved China. He considered it a war, without guns or bombs, but still a war. The virus they were using was a mutated form of a virus they stole from us, but they could not control it. That is the virus which has spread all over the world and is crippling our economy. Their plan was to infect the 'undesirables' and turn them loose on us. However, we have stopped it, with your help."

The captain turned in his seat and lifted the handset of the phone. "Pipe this through the boat." After a pause, he said, "Attention, gentlemen. I know many of you have been wondering what was happening today. We have been engaged in a top-secret mission which is now completed. I cannot tell you what the mission was about, but I can tell you this. Today we saved about a half a million American lives. You are all to be commended. That is all." From throughout the boat Chris heard cheering. The Captain broke the connection on the phone then pushed another number. When someone answered, he said, "Set a course for Pearl." He hung up.

He rose and retrieved a bottle of Scotch and four glasses from a cabinet. "Chris, are you a drinking man?"

"Only on days that end in 'Y', Captain.

CHAPTER 19

FBI Headquarters
Chicago, IL, USA
January 26, 2020
9:12 AM, Central Standard Time

Chris Weber sat at his desk for the first time in a week. Ed Martin walked into the office and said, "Hey, I thought you were going to take a few days off."

"I still have my regular duties to perform. This morning, I'm trying to review all the 302's that happened while I was lounging around in the South Pacific on our cruise with the Shanghai Lady."

Ed said, "Bobby called me this morning at zero-dark-thirty and gave me the rundown on the waves caused by the lady."

"What waves?" Chris asked.

"Everyone bought the story that she went down in the typhoon, but when all the insurance claims started coming in, someone in Beijing started to ask questions and they quickly discovered Mr. Ming's plot and were scrambling to decide who they could blame to cover their asses."

"Who did they pick?"

"Since Ming was dead and could not defend himself, he drew the short straw. He is being denounced as a rogue intelligence officer and a traitor and the United States is our friend and yada, yada, yada," Ed said. "Bobby said he had a few loose ends to tie up in China then he was coming back to Langley."

"What kind of loose ends?" Chris asked

Ed said, "He didn't say. He just said, 'loose ends'".

Chris said, "When Bobby talks about loose ends, it usually means someone is about to have some mortal problems."

"I wouldn't know, Partner", Ed said as he started to walk out. He stopped and said, "I got an email from Captain Tennyson this morning. Seems he was summoned to the White House where POTUS personally thanked him for his performance in a classified matter and promoted him to rear admiral. He said he thanked the President and whispered, "It is often a shame when a man's actions can't be mentioned because they are classified."

Across the world in Wuhan, China, Colonel Husan left the chemistry building and got into his car. As he drove home on his usual route he stopped at a red light. A motorcycle ridden by a man in a black leather outfit pulled up next to him. The driver removed a 9 mm pistol with a silencer from his jacket, fired three bullets through the side window of Husan's car, all three striking him in the head. The motorcycle sped off as Husan's car rolled out into the intersection and was struck broadside by a trolley car.

Ten minutes later, Lieutenant Ming also left the chemistry building. When he got into his car and turned the ignition key, the car exploded with a powerful blast showering shrapnel and broken glass for one hundred feet.

An hour later, General Chang, feeling he was next on the list, called Xin to fly him to his family's home in the mountains. When Chang got into the plane, he saw another man in the back seat. "Who is this?" he asked Xin.

Xin answered, "This is my cousin Bobby."

"What does he want from me?"

"He doesn't want anything. He wants to give you something," Xin said.

Quickly, Bobby leaned forward and jabbed a syringe into the side of Chang's neck. He was dead in about fifteen seconds, killed by an untraceable chemical supplied to all foreign duty officers by the CIA.

Thirty minutes later, Xin landed the plane at a small airstrip outside Beijing. He pulled into a large hangar with a larger airplane parked inside. Before he stopped moving, two men rushed from a small office toward the plane pushing a hospital gurney. Bobby and Xin got out of the plane, and the other two men went to work. They removed a blanket from the gurney, and Bobby saw a dead man dressed in one of his uniforms. "Who is that and why is he wearing my uniform?"

"That is you and he is wearing your uniform because he is you."

Xin saw the severely burned face and hands of the corpse. "Why is he burned like that?"

Bobby said, "When a plane crashes and there is a fire, the pilot, in this case you, often receives severe burns to the face and hands preventing identification. Unfortunately, you and the general were both killed in the crash which will happen shortly, and your bodies will be burned so badly that they cannot be positively identified."

As they talked, one of the men put on a parachute and climbed into the plane and took off. The plane headed toward a nearby mountain. When the pilot aimed the plane directly at the side of the mountain, he opened the door and stepped out, the parachute aiding his graceful fall to earth. The plane struck the mountain with such force, Xin could feel the shock wave at the hanger. The other man in the hanger climbed into a truck and took off toward the plane crash. In fifteen minutes, he was back at the hanger with the pilot and his parachute. Both men walked to the plane and entered it, taking the rolled-up parachute with them.

Xin asked, "What about my family?"

"Trust me," Bobby said as they walked to the large plane.

When Xin entered the plane, he found his wife and their two sons waiting for him. The children ran to Xin laughing and squealing and telling him about the plane ride they had to this place and how mother had told them to be quiet, but they could not stop their glee.

"What happens now, Bobby? What happens to us?"

"You are all dead," Bobby answered. "In a few hours, we will land at a military base in South Korea. While we are there, U. S. passports will be issued to you and your family with different names and you will be placed in what we call the witness protection program. You will be moved to some city where we will buy you a house and a car and you will start a new life in America. In a few years you will be American citizens if you want to be.

The engines started and the pilot shouted over his shoulder, "Time to leave. Everybody, buckle-up."

By the time the plane reached the runway, everyone was buckled in, even Xin's younger son, who was kicking and screaming against the restraining belt. Xin leaned over and very quietly said something to the boy who immediately became quiet and looked straight ahead.

When the plane lifted off, Bobby relaxed back into his seat and thought to himself, "God, I need a vacation."

As Bobby relaxed, in Quanzhou, China, a clean-up crew was collecting the debris left after a container ship embarked. When the crew decided to break for lunch, a peasant woman whose job was to pick up boards used to shim and level containers. She sorted the boards into two piles, reusable boards and firewood. When the rest of the crew left the area, the woman looked around to make sure she was alone. She removed a kerchief from her pocket and unwrapped her cell phone.

The woman wrote a text message to send to "The General" at a number she knew by heart. "The container ship *Eastern Sun* left the Quanzhou harbor at 0712 this date, destination unknown. The vessel contained 1,288 containers, eleven of which are owned by the Quanzhou Oriental Trading Company. Those eleven containers were loaded first and are at deck level with the doors facing outward for easy access.

The woman knew "The "General" was aware that the Quanzhou Oriental Trading Company was a front for the MSS, China's military intelligence branch. She returned to her cleaning duties.

THE END

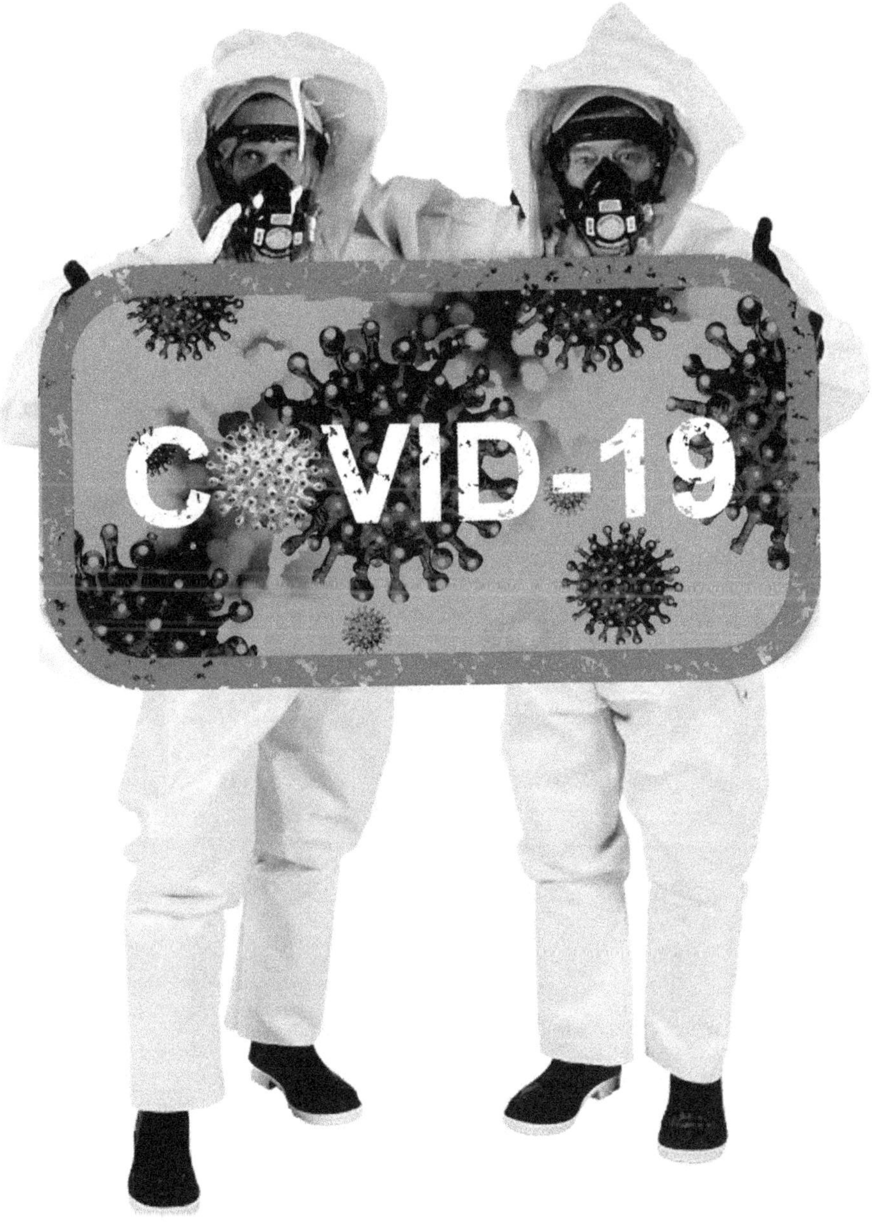
COVID-19

CPSIA information can be obtained
at www.ICGtesting.com
Printed in the USA
LVHW030434021220
673097LV00007B/334

9 781648 830662